AUGUSTUS,
THE CONQUEROR

AUGUSTUS,
THE CONQUEROR

GARY LOVISI

THE SICILLIAN: BOOK TWO

WILDSIDE PRESS

CAST OF CHARACTERS

ANDECLES—chief clerk to Roman General Agrippa.

ANDORUS—Armenian guard captain stationed inside the palace of the Armenian king.

ANON—also known as 'The Older'. Parthian slave and Roman agent who aids The Sicillian and Apollodorous.

ANON, THE YOUNGER—Another Parthian slave stationed in the palace of the Armenian king, also a Roman agent, son of Anon, who aids The Sicillian and Apollodorus in the palace with the king.

APOLLODORUS—Greek warrior and scholar, poet and killer, another agent for Caesar. Sometimes he was posed as an Athenian scholar and teacher, other times he was a warrior of Sparta. Who knew for sure. He was the mentor who raised up the Roman youth who would become The Sicillian.

CRASSUS—Roman commander and general who invaded Parthia decades in the past and was defeated, losing his army, and his legionary eagles and standards.

GAETANO SALVIDIENUS RUFUS—aka The Sicillian, youthful Roman warrior and secret agent for Caesar Augustus.

MARC ANTONY—Among other things, he was a Roman General who many years before invaded Parthia decades after the defeat of Crassus, and his legions were defeated, Antony was also the leader and present with the loss of his army, and the capture of his legionary eagles and standards.

MARCUS VIPSANIUS AGRIPPA—Roman general who was a brilliant strategist and tactician, a close friend of Caesar Augustus since they had been youths. He was totally loyal to Caesar and Rome.

MARDUS—spy and assassin who tried to murder The Sicillian in the palace of the king of Armenia.

NILUS CASCA—commander and Legate of the 12th Legion.

PHRAATES IV—the elderly King of Parthia.

SASKRA—wealthy and powerful Armenian nobleman lord, aid to the king.

TONZAT—Armenian guard captain of the outer gate to the royal palace of the king.

TRIGRANES—king of the Roman client state and buffer kingdom of Armenia in the eastern end of the Roman Empire.

XENOPHON—Parthian lord of the city of Ctesiphon, who was executed by Prince Tiridates.

XENOPHON, THE YOUNGER—son of the elder Parthian lord who had been executed by the Prince and now assumed the title.

PROLOGUE

The Parthian generals looked at their glorious master in awe and deep respect, each one waiting to hear his vaulted words as if they boomed down upon them from the gods that sat atop Mount Olympus. However, these Eastern peoples did not believe in those bastardized Greek gods, but only in Holy Mother Mithra. Mostly.

"The wheel turns once again", the Parthian prince told his generals in a firm tone, "and with it's turning there will be great changes. I have news that Caesar Augustus sends his Sicillian watchdog to give aid and cool-headed measure to his great but too-eager Roman General Agrippa," the prince told his generals, his wild eyes looked madder and more angry than usual. Those around him knew the Prince, known by some unwisely as 'The Mad Prince' and that he was a dangerous man to cross, or not to obey completely.

They obeyed him completely.

General Fareed smiled nervously, "Agrippa and his legions will have more trouble than they have bargained for out here in the East, My Prince. And yet Rome's other general, Tiberius is doing well with King Tigranes and the Armenians."

"The Armenians are dogs who shall soon know the yoke of Parthia—as their ancestors once did—before the damn Romans poked their nose into our business," the prince growled. He knew that once Armenia had been a part of his father's empire and was due to Parthia by Devine Right.

Takir, the First General added confidently to assuage the prince's mood, "It shall not do Augustus, nor Agrippa, any good should this one man come here. What can one man do? Nothing! And we shall take care of the whelp Tiberius. He is but one more Roman. The die is cast here in Parthia and it is foretold that Rome shall meet it's doom here in the East in a coming great battle. It will be a war like no other. Caesar wants it—and it shall be Rome's doom, just as it was twice in the past with Crassus and Antony. Two arrogant Roman fools—soon we shall add one more defeated Roman army and general to that list."

The Parthian prince smiled now, anticipating the coming conflagration. It would truly be terrible, hundreds of thousands would die. He shrugged, so be it. He could always raise more troop levies, ore soldiers, but he could not create more land for Parthia. That had to be fought for and paid for in blood. So be it.

The prince spoke up, "Yes, I agree, but this Sicillian could cause us a problem. He is known to be trouble. He is a catalyst for Roman action and activity which we do not want—and he brings with him clear-headed thinking which we do not want the Romans to have in this matter. I have heard news of his recent activities as far away as *Hispania* from some of our agents there, Roman traitors who are in my employ. They call themselves Liberators. I think it best that this Sicillian be waylaid and eliminated before he ever meets with Agrippa. I do not want to have any interference by him here that might lessen our prospects for success in this venture should these two Roman generals meet and join their forces. I feel that this Sicillian is a key man in this venture, he is a trusted messenger of Caesar, so who knows what valuable information he may be privy to."

Takir nodded sagely "Yes, of course, My Prince, yet, I have heard Agrippa is not overly fond of this Sicillian."

"True, that is well known, but if you can not kill him, perhaps we can catch him and then find out all he knows. Under our interrogators I can promise he will give up everything he knows," the Prince added with a dark grim smile of anticipation. He had been present on many of these types of 'interrogations' in the past and he had enjoyed them immensely.

General Fareed now spoke up softly, carefully, "That may be true, and I have also heard the converse of that axiom, something else we might consider. I have it on good source that this Sicillian is not fond of Agrippa, they may even be enemies. We can use that, My Lord."

The Prince nodded once again, "Yet both are true and loyal servants of Caesar Augustus. We know this to be true as well. I believe that unites them, and makes them stronger than their dislike of each other. We do not need them to join forces now."

"No, My Lord," the Generals all agreed.

The Parthian prince nodded regally, "Then it is settled, my brothers. General Fareed, take some of our scouts and see to it that this Sicillian, whoever he may be, never meets with General Agrippa. Can you arrange that?"

The general smiled wickedly, "the Roman dog is as good as dead, My Prince."

"Good, then raise the tribal armies, and let each local leader and governor know that the orders for troop arrival shall be strictly enforced," the prince told them firmly, and his generals smiled, for they knew what that meant.

Tribal armies here in the East were raised very quickly from local levies, and because the last man who arrived was tortured to death in front of the entire army, it proved to be a powerful incentive for the men to arrive quickly when the king or any prince called. So they all ran with all speed when the king or any of his governors called them to arms! As if their very lives depended upon it!

CHAPTER I

The Roman Republic was Gone.

Lost.

A memory now.

The Empire has replaced it.

Strong.

Bold.

Roman!

The man known as The Sicillian, Gaetano Salvidienus Rufus, or just plain Rufus, looked keenly at the message he had received from his friend and mentor, the wily Greek warrior scholar Apollodorus—another agent of the great Caesar Augustus.

The message told Rufus all he needed to know about the Roman legion eagles and standards that had been held captive by the Parthians for so many years. Caesar wanted those military icons returned to Roman control and The Sicillian was ordered by him to see that they were swiftly and safely returned to Rome—and to Caesar.

One way—or another!

It was a seemingly impossible mission.

The Sicillian knew that to achieve his mission he would have to work with the victorious Roman General Agrippa, who had assembled a vast Roman army in the East—so that one way or the other—the two men could accomplish this task for Rome and Caesar. That meant it would be achieved either by diplomacy and reason—or by war and blood. But Rufus and Agrippa, while being totally loyal to Caesar—and each of them being the best and truest of his friends—did not overly like each other. In fact, there was much suspicion and distrust between The Sicillian and Caesar's vaulted General Agrippa—but that being said, they each served Caesar Augustus with all their heart and that was all that mattered to these two men for now. Their loyalty and service to Caesar was always their goal. So it would be now, and so it would be on this mission as well.

To victory or death!

Gaetano Salvidienus Rufus, the man known now as The Sicillian, rode his black Batavian war steed quickly towards the edge of the eastern Roman Empire on a secret mission for Great Caesar. He rode swiftly and with purpose for his mission was of vast importance and he would not allow delay or failure. He could never allow failure—and neither would Caesar Augustus allow him to fail. He knew he had only a limited amount of time to perform what could only be pulled off as a miracle. If not, then things would spiral out of hand.

The three riders who followed behind The Sicillian on the easterly road moved up fast and with deadly intent. They were dressed as common men of arms from the eastern lands—certainly not Roman—and more than likely they were mere bandits or thieves looking to make an easy haul on a single lone traveler. However, there could be more to these three riders than met the eye. Perhaps.

Meeting that type of ruffian was a common occurrence on these well-made eastern roads. Roads and bridges built by conquering Roman legions, but these days out here in the wilds of the far East, the roads were not so widely patrolled as they used to be by legionary soldiers. For General Agrippa had called in all centuries and cohorts into his vast army that now sat on the border of the Roman buffer kingdom of Armenia like a giant tiger poised to strike the Parthian snake.

Meanwhile, Caesar's heroic young general, Tiberius, moved south with more legions ready to strike. But Caesar had made it plain that while he was open to negotiation and diplomacy in the matter of the return of the lost legionary eagles and standards, he was also just as ready to spill blood to take them back by force, if need be. Rufus, The Sicillian, was one of two men instructed by Caesar to bring about an impossible task out here in the East. Without causing another war.

The Sicillian rode ever onward and eastwards. He gave his horse a significant kick and the swift Batavian steed spurned onwards down the well-hewn Roman stone-paved road. The three men following behind the Roman also quickened the speed of their mounts and soon began to close up on the lone rider. The Sicillian knew what was to come, he prepared himself, and slowed his mount and waited. He did not have long to wait. He wanted to get this over with as soon as possible—and he knew that it would be concluded soon, one way or another.

The charge of the three men came as a fast sudden attack. The three mysterious riders spurring their horses towards the lone man waiting patiently on his steady and barely moving huge warhorse.

The Sicillian gripped the *pilum* from his pack, he hefted the deadly Roman javelin with the heavy metal pointed head, testing it's balance and readying it for a true throw as the three mounted men now charged down upon him.

"Drop your weapon, Roman! We are only after your gold, not your life. Surrender to us and you shall go free," the leader told the Roman, appealing to what he thought was common sense. The man already had a wicked-looking sword out and pointed at the Roman, and his two fellows also had their swords out and ready.

The Sicillian laughed. He knew only too well that whether thief or assassin, it was always the plan of such creatures to leave no witness alive after they had done their dirty deed.

Though the leader of the charging attackers said he was merely a thief who was only after gold, the man looked like an skilled assassin, and The Sicillian still had recent memories of Milo the Praetorian and his men, who he had met and bested months back in Gaul. He had the same feeling about these three rogues—thieves perhaps?—but they could just as easily be assassins as well. If so, then be it so. He was ready for them!

The three attackers charged fully upon the lone Roman who turned his steed, took aim and let loose with his javelin. The *pilum* flew through the air guided by it's heavy metal pointed head, to imbed itself deeply into the chest of the attacking rider on the left. The man screamed in bloody rage and then fell from his horse and was dead, or mortally wounded. In any case he was out of action, immediately. Rufus would take care of him later, he would not be a threat for now. Right now he had the other two men to contend with, so he quickly drew his *gladius*, the short Roman fighting sword of the legions, and awaited the remaining two riders to close with him. They were upon him quickly.

"Well done, Roman, taking out my man, but you shall not get away from the two of us that easily!" the leader of the duo shouted in anger.

"Then come closer and taste my blade!" The Sicillian shouted back in defiant rage.

The two attackers came at the Roman with their swords drawn, one from each side, trying to outflank him and get through his guard. Rufus knew their tactic and he quickly fought them off, twisted his body, as he guided his mount effectively to blunt their hard attack. His warhorse, being as much a veteran of battle was it's rider, knew how to maneuver in the press of battle without too much instruction from it's rider.

The blades of his attackers came down upon the Roman again and again—and missed again and again, as The Sicillian blunted their blade with his own sharp strokes and wove a pathway through their guard. Hard blows were struck by both sides for long moments. The area echoed with the loud clang and pounding of hard metal swordplay. Then Rufus was able to catch the first man with a quick feint, slashing him with a deep cut in the throat. The man loudly cried out and then gurgled in shock as blood gushed out and upwards, his head fell back, and then he dropped down from his horse to the ground. The wounded attacker's horse ran off and now that was one more enemy out of action. There was only one left now, the leader of the attackers.

The Sicillian turned to face that leader of the broken trio now—it was much better odds—one on one.

"Not so sure of yourself are you now?" The Sicillian shouted out as he pressed his attack on his remaining lone adversary. The two war horses turned around and clashed into one another, as the men atop them clashed at each other with loud clanging swords viciously hacking down upon one another, each looking for an opening to cut his adversary down.

The Sicillian's enemy was the leader of the trio of attackers and he proved a better fighter than his mates, but he was still no match for the Roman. The Sicillian used his war steed to push into and force the attacker's mount to change position and when he had done that, Rufus surged forward and was able to plunge his blade into the man's chest, through his chain mail armor, and deeply into or near his vitals. Perhaps right into his heart. No, not his heart, for the man still lived—though barely. The thief leader was powerfully knocked off his horse and onto the ground by the blow. The man lay there and did not move.

The Sicillian rode over and quickly dismounted his steed and went over to the man before he expired from his wound. The attacker was obviously dying and would surely be dead soon. Rufus knew he did not have much time.

"Thief, you and your friends have gotten what you deserved!" Rufus told the dying man. "Now speak up and tell me who sent you!"

The man growled, angry he was dying and that he and his men had been bested by this one young man whom he had been told would be little trouble at all. "You… you were supposed to be easy prey."

"Me? No, not easy prey, my friend," The Sicillian told him with a grim smile.

"No, the vaulted Sicillian, you are said to be the agent of the Caesar of the Romans. I should have known."

Rufus looked hard at the dying man then, "So you know who I am. How do you know that? How do you know of my connection with Caesar! Speak up man!" and the Roman grabbed the dying man roughly, in an effort to make him speak up before he died. "Give up your secret now, assassin!"

The Sicillian knew now that these men were assassins and not mere thieves as he had first supposed, and as they had intended him to believe.

"Speak up!" The Sicillian demanded gruffly, shaking the man, but by then he had bled out and was already dead, a grim mocking rectus of a death smile upon his face. He had not given up any information to the Roman.

"Damned assassin!" The Sicillian growled and then he let the man's body drop to the ground. He cleaned the blood off his sword on the dead man's tunic, then sheathed his weapon and looked upon the man more closely. Not a Roman. No, but that did not mean anything by itself, all kinds of men were available for hire and all kinds took the call of the assassin for the right price in gold. But this encounter was troubling, and adding to it his previous encounter with the Praetorian assassin Milo in Gaul, it was a serious danger. He knew he was on someone's death list—but whose? He knew that things were heating up and that news of his mission here in the East for Caesar had somehow gotten out to the enemy—to whoever his enemy might be.

The Sicillian nodded, accepting the risk, it went with the mission. So be it. He took some time and carefully looked over each of the three men he had just killed for any indication of who they might be, where they were from, or who they might be working for. Their weapons were a motley assortment of deadly blades from various nations, including Roman. He found Parthian gold in their pocket pouches, each man had a small group of gold coins, prominently stamped with the image of the Parthian king, Phraates IV. This then, must have been their payment for his murder, but the fact that their payment was in Parthian gold did not necessarily mean that these men worked for the king of that enemy empire. Perhaps yes, but perhaps no? It was a perplexing issue and since The Sicillian could find no other evidence to move forward any theory—such as a most convenient papyrus scroll or wax tablet giving the order for his murder—there was nothing more to do now but re-mount his horse and be on his way. He left the bodies of the three men where they had fallen. He had no desire to bury them but he did relieve each of them of their gold. Where they were going—down into deep dark Hades he hoped—they would have no need of any gold.

Then he rode onward.

CHAPTER II

"The East!"

"The place is a damnable sewer where we—Rome—end up getting sucked down into the mire every time we come out here," General Marcus Vipsanius Agrippa stated grimly, showing his anger at the Parthians, to his legion commanders. These were the legates, tribunes, and cohort centurions whose jurisdiction held sway over the most eastern end of the Roman Empire. The Eastern Frontier. All important men. All fully loyal to Caesar Augustus—but out here in the far East that meant one man—Caesar's most loyal trusted representative and general—Agrippa.

The General sighed, looked around him at the throng of officers present at the meeting. They were all good men, and good Romans, able commanders, and their legions were well-honed fighting machines—as taut and deadly as any ballista or catapult—and ready to be let loose to reign terror upon the enemies of Rome. Agrippa had always had a love of the artillery and he used it well.

The General stood up tall and proud, for though he was not an overly tall man—as most true Romans were—he was certainly proud. Despite his lack of height he appeared to be taller than he actually was. He was powerful. Well-built. A proud Roman and a loyal one—loyal to Caesar Augustus. The two men had been friends since childhood with good memories and where loyalty had been tested many times.

"We are met here because our emissaries to the damned Parthians came back without any resolution to our demands," Agrippa forcefully pronounced, letting his commanders know he was unhappy with them and the results so far out here in the eastern end of the Empire.

Nilus Casca stood up, he was the legate of the 12th Legion, "General, these damned savages… These Parthians have ever been a thorn in the side of Rome and they are doing so now. Your request is simple enough."

"My request?" Agrippa stated, "It is Caesar's request. A Demand!"

"These easterners are purposefully being obstinate to prick us as they always do," one of the younger tribunes spoke up, a bit out of turn, he had little battle experience but he was from a powerful influential family with political connections, so he felt he could voice his concerns freely here at this meeting. Not always a wise thing to do.

Agrippa said nothing but he was annoyed by the tribune's remark, but the other legates there gave the young tribune stony looks of disapproval.

"You speak out of turn!" Casca firmly reminded the young tribune.

"Enough! Caesar wants his damn eagles and standards returned," Agrippa spoke up fiercely now. He looked out hard at all the men in that room. All grizzled veterans of the wars with the murderers of the Devine Julius, and then the later battles with the traitor Marc Antony, and that Egyptian witch, Cleopatra. Agrippa looked at them harshly. "Tiberius has already made a name for himself out in Syria—and he is but 21 years of age."

"Aye, Tiberius shows great promise," one commander nodded sagely, admiring the younger general's courage and accomplishments attained at such a youthful age. And he was the nephew of Augustus Caesar.

"He is an up and comer, I'll give him that," another said plainly.

"Yes," another officer agreed, "if he can stay alive long enough to prove his worth."

"Oh, that one shall survive, he has a cold heart and a bloody sword for the enemies of Caesar—and a sharp mind for strategy and tactics. He serves Caesar well."

"As we all shall do, shall we not?" Agrippa put it to the assemblage.

The men there all nodded enthusiastically, not out of any lackey response, for these were true believers in the righteousness of Rome and Augustus—and both empire and man meant the same to each of these men. Equally were Rome and Caesar revered in their thoughts, the noble Agrippa knew.

"So what shall we do?" another of the legates asked cautiously. "What are your orders, General? Do we invade Parthia, take their lands, lay siege to their cities? Our army out here is small to go up against their vast hordes which far outnumber our own. My spies tell me the Prince has called up all the tribal armies as well. Also, our supply lines would be stretched dangerously thin should any war begin before we are fully ready."

"Yes, I know the facts of the situation we face here only too well," Agrippa admitted with a grimace of impatience, "but I promised Caesar Augustus those lost legionary eagles and standards, and he shall get them, if it takes me another year of useless haggling with these damned Parthians—or if it leads to outright war. They are a slippery lot to deal with."

"Damned savages!" one officer added adamantly.

"Barbarians! Slippery as a snake," another made his feelings on the matter known.

"Insulting them will not win them over or force them to accept our demands," Legate Nilus Casca of the 12th Legion spoke up once again.

"Casca is correct, gentlemen," Agrippa admitted reluctantly, holding down his impatient anger. He wanted to begin the war now and get this all over with. It was inevitable, after all, that the two great empires that ruled the world would fight one grand war for final dominance. Agrippa was sure who would win that war—Rome. He nodded, then continued, "but Caesar wants those eagles and standards returned to Rome and he shall have them if we have to be posted out here for another year—or even longer. He will put pressure on the Parthians, put pressure on them and also their client states. He is sending another emissary. A rider is on his way to Tigranes, the king of the Armenians, who will send us one of his know-nothing princes with a long and impressive name that means nothing—as a hostage. We shall send Caesar's man to the Parthian court—one snake to speak sweet bent words to another. Perhaps we shall get some response then? I will allow it if it works, but I am for war now, right away. It is only Caesar who holds me back for now! So that is how it shall be played for the present! That is all."

"Is there any other business?" Andecles, Agrippa's chief clerk addressed the group of officers.

No one replied. They fully understood the situation.

"Then this meeting is concluded," Agrippa said with a wry grimace. He knew the man he was sending out today was not an Armenian at all, but a Greek, another agent for Caesar, a man he did not trust named Apollodorus. The General ordered his clerk, "Have that 'Armenian' prince brought to me as soon as he gets here. I have very specific instructions for him."

Gaetano Salvidienus Rufus, known in Rome and parts West as The Sicillian, rode his trusty black Batavian warhorse through the rocky lands of the eastern end of the Roman Empire. Out here, it was a strange foreign world for most Romans, the end of the world in many aspects. It was a land inhabited by strange and fierce peoples with savage and barbarian customs and habits. A world very un-Roman—and yet a world that seemed ripe for the plucking for Rome to conquer. A vast area ripe for new Roman victories. If the people would cooperate. They would not. They were a stubborn lot. However, this was a part of the world that was brimming with riches and wealth. It was a perfect place for Rome to take for her own—but for the damned Parthians. They had always been a threat and a problem. They were proving so now. A forever thorn in the side of Rome's eastern expansion and desire for great wealth.

The Sicillian rode onwards towards a small village in Syria. It was a desert land, hot and sunny, yet fertile in some places with good farm land and happy people. It was a good land for Rome to have under it's sway. And it was rich. Full of wealth in many forms. Rufus knew this from his friend and tutor, the Greek scholar and warrior, Apollodorus, who had prepared him back in Rome for this mission.

That mission was on the Roman's mind now. A seemingly impossible duty ordered by Caesar for him to accomplish—to meet with the hated Parthians and to secure the release of the Roman legionary eagles and standards that had fallen to the Parthians in military defeats many years ago. The loss was a stain upon Rome that Caesar sought to remedy, even at the threat of war in the East. The Sicillian was under no illusions how difficult his task would be. For he knew that Caesar had also sent out his most able general and loyal friend, Agrippa, who was here with an army to treaty with, threaten, bribe, and even make war on the dread Parthians to get those eagles and standards returned. So far Agrippa had tried diplomacy and met with failure.

Now Caesar had sent Rufus, The Sicillian, to aid his most able general in this undertaking. It would not go easily. The Parthians knew that Caesar Augustus was frantic to have those eagles and standards returned, so they were making it a most difficult situation. King Tigranes, of the Roman client state of Armenia—supposedly a neutral buffer between the eastern end of the Empire and the Parthians was the man that The Sicillian was to see first—before he reported to General Agrippa—but Agrippa it seemed had his own plans.

The road had been long and dusty and eventually the lands of Syria became the lands of Armenia, the Roman client state that was a buffer between two vast empires. Tigranes was the king here, a Roman puppet who seemed a complex man—or perhaps just a man playing a complex game—and The Sicillian made for his city and palace. On his person he held a secret medallion given to him by Caesar Augustus himself to present to Tigranes as proof of his office of Imperial Roman Emissary. *Sub rosa.*

Rufus rode into the capital city and towards the Armenian palace, through the streets of this bustling eastern land. It was a lovely city, taking it's design much after the Babylonian and Assyrian architecture of ages before, but with much Greek influence as well in the buildings and in the clothing of the people.

The Sicillian rode through the crowded streets packed with colorfully dressed men and women. He was not stopped or even questioned, which seemed odd to him, being a stranger in that city. And an obvious foreigner. In fact, he seemed to be barely noticed at all, but he noticed the people. He saw men whose jet black hair and beards were strung in curling ringlets of oiled elaborate designs. The women had long hair piled high in even more elaborate designs, jet black, with painted faces and colorful eastern clothing. It was most interesting and very unlike what one saw in Rome—unless one roamed in the foreign quarters. And yet, here was a bustling and wealthy city. A plum prize for sure. It was also at peace. For the present. Under Roman protection. Not fearing the Parthians. Not fearing Rome. The Sicillian wondered about that and what game the Armenians were playing out here in the East. It was probably a simple one, he surmised, a game called survival— when a small state is snuggly situated between two large and powerful belligerent ones. Or so the warrior sage Apollodorus had warned him weeks ago.

"Be careful of the Parthians, my boy," the wily old Greek had told his young charge back then, "but he especially careful of the Armenians and their ruler, this Tigranes. I trust him not."

The Sicillian thought about all that now as he guided his black Batavian warhorse down the avenues of the Armenian capitol. He had not been challenged at the main gate by any soldiers, nor on any of the city streets, but as he approached the royal palace he was halted at the gate by an officer of the guard and his men. While rules and security seemed lax in the city, they seemed to be more serious here at the palace. As its should be.

"You have reached the palace of Tigranes, King of Armenia, what business do you have here, Roman?" the guard officer asked him bluntly.

"So you see I am Roman?" The Sicillian offered.

"I see you are Roman, yet still my question stands," the officer insisted, his men moving closer to him, some with hands slowly moving to the hilts of their swords.

"I seek an audience with your king," the Roman spoke up. "I am called The Sicillian, and I bring word to him from Rome and from Great Caesar Augustus himself."

The guard commander thought mightily about this for a moment, then said, "And you have some evidence to prove this?"

"Yes, but it is for the eyes of your king only," Rufus replied firmly. His hand was upon the hilt of his own short *gladius* now as well. He was ready—if need be to fight it out.

"That presents us with a problem, my Roman friend. For you know we Armenians are friends to Rome, but here in the East, assassins are often found under every bed and bush. You must prove to me you are an emissary of Caesar before I allow you into the palace grounds, much less anywhere near our king."

"I understand. Then do you know of your Lord Saskra?"

"Of course, a noblemen of great wealth and influence with the king."

"Then call him here and he will vouch for me. Tell him The Sicillian has come from Rome and seeks his company now, and have him brought here and all shall be explained."

The guard officer shook his head dubiously, "The noble lord is not one I can order about, and certainly not for the likes of you."

"Yes, that may well be true...unless I be actually from Caesar. Then your fat will surely be in the fire if you do not tell your king that I am here," The Sicillian responded quickly with a sharpness to his tone that got the captain's attention. And got the man thinking.

The guard officer nodded slowly, thinking it through some more, then called over one of his men, gave him a quick order, and the man ran off.

"Quarles will seek out Lord Saskra, who is in the palace and likely with the king. I am sure he will come here soon. So now, we wait, Roman."

"Yes, we wait," The Sicillian replied, getting down from his mount and taking a drink from his water skin. He offered a drink to the guard captain, and the man took a welcome drink of not water—but sweet watered wine. Most welcomed by the officer, who gave his thanks.

"So you are out from Rome?" the officer asked Rufus by way of conversation. News from travelers, especially out from Rome was always worthy of hearing.

"Yes," Rufus replied bluntly.

"A long way to travel."

"Yes, it is."

"So what is the news from Rome?"

"The same. Rome is as it always is, and always was."

"Hah! That tells me much and nothing," the officer stated showing his disappointment in not being allowed to hear some worthy news or juicy gossip.

"That is ever the way in Rome these days, my Armenian friend."

"We are Roman here too, you know. It is not easy with the damned Parthians breathing down our necks."

"I would have thought otherwise, my friend," The Sicillian replied with a wary look.

"Ah, yes, I see what you mean. Yes, we have them here too. Men who only look out for themselves and their own interests at the expense of Armenia and our king."

"And of Rome?" The Sicillian asked.

"Yes, and of Rome as well."

"And these others?" he prompted the guard captain.

The officer smiled, "Yes, Roman, we have them here in abundance, spies, rogues, even traitors."

"And where do you fit in, my friend?" he asked the Armenian officer, looking the man firmly in the eyes.

"Loyal to my country and my king, which means I am loyal to Rome as well—and Caesar," the officer replied, almost proudly.

"Ah, now that is good to hear, Captain."

" Yes, and by now Parthian ears have not only heard our words, but are busy reporting them back to the Prince of Parthia, and his point man here in Armenia, General Fareed."

"Yes, I have heard of Fareed," The Sicillian replied.

"Yes, and he has probably heard of you and is putting men on your trail right now, Roman."

He knew that had already probably happened. The three men he had fought with on the road. It might happen again.

The Sicillian allowed a grim smile, then said, "Good, then I shall welcome them with this…" and he put his hand meaningfully on his scabbarded *gladius* short sword.

The captain responded thoughtfully, looking at the Roman sword carefully, "Shorter than our eastern swords, and not curved, but I have heard it is a truly deadly weapon."

"In the proper hands, it can be devastating."

Then the guard captain's attention was taken by a newly arrived officer who gave him a secret signal.

"Come with me and my men now, Roman, into the palace, to meet our king. I have just been given the approval, and King Tigranes, and Lord Saskra, wish to see you immediately."

"Lead on, Captain," The Sicillian replied as he followed the men. "And what is your name, good fellow?"

"I am called Tonzat, and I have the honor to be Captain of the Outer Gate of the Royal Palace of Tigranes—King and Lord of all Armenia."

"That is certainly a mouthful, my friend," the Roman laughed. He derided long loutish titles.

"Yes, it is meant to be impressive to visitors and strangers, but I am afraid we Armenians—struck between Parthia and Rome are trapped into playing a most precarious game."

"Then best make certain you are on the winning side," The Sicillian told Captain Tonzat.

"That is ever our aim, my friend."

"And Rome is the winning side."

"For the moment, Roman," Tonzat replied with a grim smile.

"Then lead on, Captain Tonzat and I shall give my message to your king from Great Caesar."

Captain Tonzat led The Sicillian into and through the royal palace accompanied by his troop of guards. They escorted him to the huge doors that were opened to show a long and elaborate throne room.

"Here I must leave you, Roman," the captain told him in a friendly manner. "Good luck and have a care, the vipers here make the snakes of our grim deserts pale by comparison."

"Not unlike Rome, itself, my friend," The Sicillian replied with a wry grin. "I appreciate your candor, and the warning."

Then Captain Tonzat ordered his troop away as a new officer approached with his own guard troop from the palace. These were inner palace guards, much better dressed and better equipped.

"Roman, I am Captain Andorus, and we shall escort you to the throne of King Tigranes."

"Then lead on," The Sicillian replied.

"First your sword, My Lord. You must give it up," Andorus insisted. "It is only a temporary measure, I assure you."

The Sicillian nodded understanding the situation, and he slowly and carefully handed over his *gladius* to the throne room captain.

"Good," the Captain responded. "Now follow me."

The Sicillian walked into the huge and richly appointed throne room of the Armenian king. The place was a treasure trove of golden statues and precious impressive tapestries along with grand works of art, all of which was so intricately detailed and richly made in the Eastern style. They were prominently displayed works. There was great wealth here and The Sicillian instantly understood why both Rome and Parthia sought to add this buffer kingdom to their own empires. Rome had won that struggle—so far. Would she continue to control the kingdom? It was anyone's guess.

The Sicillian was escorted to the far end of the chamber where a rather youngish man sat upon a golden throne. That would be Tigranes, King of Armenia. At his side stood another man, older, very well dressed and with much jewelry, obviously some advisor or such. This would turn out to be the Lord Saskra he had heard about.

The Sicillian was led forward, unarmed now, by Captain Andorus and his men. He was brought before Tigranes and the other man who stood by on the right side of the King's throne.

"King Tigranes of Armenia," the guard captain informed the Roman. "My king, this Roman says he is a messenger from Caesar Augustus."

"Bring him forward," commanded the king.

"I bring a coin, oh, King, given to me by Caesar Augustus himself, to present to you to prove my identity," The Sicillian explained.

The king nodded.

"Carefully, Roman," the guard captain warned.

The Sicillian nodded, then slowly, and carefully withdrew the coin, and then handed it to the captain, who presented it to his King.

Tigranes looked the silver coin over carefully, nodded knowingly, then gave it back to his captain to return to the Roman.

"Yes, Sicillian, I was told of your journey out East, you bare the seal of Augustus. Know that it was General Marcus Vipsanius Agrippa, who under Caesar's orders and direction, had me set upon the throne of Armenia. So I am loyal to Rome and Caesar. Not to mention that General Agrippa still has his army—of many legions—on the border of my nation with Parthia. Meanwhile I have news that Tribune and General Tiberius, the teenage stepson of Caesar Augustus, has lately arrived in southern Syria with another army poised upon the border with Parthia," the king looked around him at the man at his side. He nodded, then added, "Does Caesar intend to have these two armies invade Parthia?"

The Sicillian thought upon this for a serious moment, for he knew he had to be careful about what he said now, and what he did not say. He nodded, allowed a wry grin, "That, oh king, is a most difficult question to answer, for you know that Great Caesar Augustus desires above all things peace—but there is the matter of the return to him of his lost legionary eagles and standards. The property of Rome. That is most important and preys upon his mind."

"Even above extending the Empire's boundaries?" the king asked bluntly.

"Yes, I believe that to be so," The Sicillian replied firmly and, as far as he knew, truthfully.

"That is a lie!" the man at the king's side spoke up loud and boldly for the first time.

"My Lord Saskra seems to feel otherwise," the king offered, allowing his own concern to show now.

The Sicillian took a deep breath, shrugged, as if the Lord's suspicions were insignificant. "Who can be sure of such things, oh King? All I can tell you is that I was tasked with the mission by Caesar to see to it that the eagles and standards were returned to their rightful owners from the Parthians. It is only justice, after so many years. I was told by Caesar himself to seek you out and that you would aid me in this quest being a true friend of Rome."

The King of the Armenians nodded thoughtfully, but he did not overly like being placed in between any problems of Rome and Parthia. He finally offered up a dour grimace. "I am a true and loyal friend to Rome, but I do not know what I can do to help you in this mission,

Sicillian. I have no powers over the man who sits upon the Parthian throne, nor the young prince who it is said is the true power behind that throne."

"And a prince who hates Rome with a passion," Lord Saskra added to complete the difficulties of the Roman's mission.

"He does?"

"Most assuredly," both king and lord agreed.

"I see," The Sicillian added thoughtfully. That presented added difficulties. What to do? He looked around the throne room at the King, at Lord Saskra, even over at Captain Andorus and his men. They were alone now. Captain Andorus held The Sicillian's *gladius*—for safekeeping. For the moment. He did not like that situation at all now. Unarmed. Were these men truly friends of Rome?

"So what of this prince of the Parthians," the Roman envoy asked.

King Tigranes spoke up, "He is Tiridates, the elder son of the old Parthian King Phraates IV. A most volatile young fellow, difficult to deal with. He will become king of Parthia some day—if he is not murdered in his sleep, or does not kill himself with excess—and you Romans think you have a thorn in your side with Parthia now! You have no idea what lies upon the horizon if Prince Tiridates ascends to the throne."

"So then he must not ascend to the throne," The Sicillian spoke up. It was not a question.

"Oh, I believe he shall rule Parthia soon, Roman," Lord Saskra spoke up firmly, confidently! "You Romans shall not have too long to wait."

The Sicillian nodded, he had listened to the Armenian lords words most carefully—and that was all he needed to know. For now he knew that his mission in the East had taken on one more aspect for Caesar. A duty he must perform, if it was possible, one that he now added to his original mission. He knew Caesar would want it done. That mission was that the Parthian prince, Tiridates, must die!

The Sicillian looked carefully at the men in that huge throne room. Who could he trust? Who was truly loyal to Caesar and Rome? Were any of them? They all proclaimed that they were loyal to Rome in the most strong language, but that meant nothing. Empty words? Perhaps?

"We shall aid you in your quest, Roman." King Tigranes spoke up with a slight nod of his head. "Allow my guard to escort you to a chamber to rest from your long journey. Sup with me this evening and you shall be given what information I possess to aid you in achieving your mission for Caesar."

"I thank you, King Tigranes," the Roman emissary spoke up as he was led away to what turned out to be a rather lavish chamber inside the palace. Here Captain Andorus and his men would leave him. Before the captain left, he held out something, "Here is your short sword, Roman."

"I thank you," and The Sicillian deftly sheathed the deadly weapon in his scabbard.

"You will have need of it, I am sure," the captain warned the Roman. "I will come for you as sunset approaches. Be ready. You will find all you need here to bathe and make yourself presentable. Slaves will come in to take care of all your needs."

"Thank you, again," The Sicillian told Captain Andorus.

The captain allowed a knowing smile, "Do not thank me too readily, Roman. You have entered a nest of vipers here, and I do not envy your position—even if you be a Roman."

The Sicillian nodded knowingly, "I thank you regardless."

"Hah!" Captain Andorus spoke up with an ironic laugh and then left as he voiced a gruff order and led his men away.

CHAPTER III

Gaetano Salvidienus Rufus, known as The Sicillian, was attended to by various slaves who bathed him and washed the grime of travel and of the roads off his body. In the meantime other slaves washed and cleaned his tunic and uniform, shined his armor and sword, washed his war cloak and boots, so that he was soon most presentable and once again dressed in his own comfortable red legionary tunic that were for once cleaned as if newly made. It was a wonder and made him feel ready to meet King Tigranes and his court, and Lord Saskra, or anyone else here in the East who he must deal with. Chief among them, he knew now, was that Roman-hating prince of the Parthians, as well as his own Roman commander of the Empire's military forces out here in the East, General Marcus Agrippa.

The Sicillian and General Agrippa did not get along. There was often some manner of dislike and distrust among them, but both men were steadfastly loyal to Caesar and so both worked together to serve the leader they both admired and respected. Agrippa had been a most trusted youthful friend of Caesar going back many years. Rufus, also considered himself a friend to Caesar—and Caesar to be a friend to him—as long as the Roman leader did not find out about the relationship between his sister, Octavia, and himself. Caesar Augustus would never approve of that relationship. And that got him to thinking about his beloved Octavia and when he would see her again. It would be some time, he feared. He missed her and thought of her often, but there was nothing to do about any of that now. She was half a world away back in Rome, doing—- what? Meanwhile he was out here in the armpit of the Empire. Who even knew if he would win through this mission with his life?

The Sicillian shrugged, there was nothing to do about it now, so he got himself ready for the supper feast—a time of grand eating and drinking in the palace—and over-eating and over-drinking—but a gathering when many plans and alliances were often discussed and set in motion. An important gathering.

Rufus was just about to leave his suite of rooms when a new servant entered the chamber. This was a different man than those he had seen before—he was large and beefy—but appearing almost silently. He did not look like any common slave. If anything, he appeared to have once been a solider, or more likely, even a gladiator. The Roman was immediately suspicious of the fellow, but then put it all down to the vagaries of a slave's manner among the master class.

"I was sent to escort you to the King, My Lord," the burly servant told him in a gruff voice that did not seem servant-like at all. The man was armed with his own *gladius*, which seemed strange to The Sicillian here inside the palace of Tigranes, but then again, he had been allowed to wear his own *gladius* now, so he put it from his mind at the moment. Obviously if the slave was allowed to go around armed, he must have the permission of the king.

"I am ready. What is your name?" Rufus asked the man.

The servant seemed to think upon that for a moment, then smiled and said, "I am called Mardus. Now follow me."

Mardus led The Sicillian out of the chamber and into a long, rather secluded hallway.

"Is this the way to the King's throne room?"

"No, the King is having his revelry in the grand banquet hall, on the other side of the palace. That is why he sent me here to escort you. The palace is very large and it is easy for one not accustomed to the place to find himself to become lost. It would not do for you to become lost, or be late, for the King's banquet."

The Sicillian nodded, that all seemed quite plausible, but still his hand moved across to the left side of his body to grasp the pommel of his short sword. It was well that he did so.

"Down that hall, Roman," Mardus told The Sicillian in a softer tone. "Walk on ahead of me, over there to the large doors at the end of this hallway. They are all awaiting you there."

The Sicillian looked at the large doors, ostensively leading to a grand banquet hall, but with no other people in view, nor even any outside guards to indicate that anyone was there. It did not seem right and The Sicillian grew cautious. Or was he just being overly suspicious? He looked closely at Mardus, but the man's face was an unmovable mask. This entire scheme did not seem right to the Roman—in fact it seemed that this Mardus fellow had led him into a secluded section of the palace that could prove perfect for an ambush, or an assassination.

It seemed impossible, but there the thought came into his mind—and none too soon.

The Sicillian quickly drew his *gladius*, turned, and in a swift motion, was able to duck and ward off the glancing blow that suddenly came from behind down upon him from the sword held in the hand of Mardus.

"Bloody assassin!" The Sicillian growled and used his sword to come back at his attacker with a bold stroke that forced the man back a bit.

Mardus had somehow silently withdrawn his own weapon and had been ready to cut down the Roman—had Rufus not turned in time to stop him. Some sixth sense of the fighting man had caused Rufus to draw his own sword to counter the brain crunching blow of Mardus. So now the battle began.

The two men clashed weapons wildly in that long, dark and secluded hallway. The Sicillian instantly realized that this Mardus was an able fighter, good with a sword, and that he had in fact once been a gladiator—for he surely fought like one.

However, there was a big difference between a gladiator and a solider of the legions. Far often a gladiator could best a simple soldier—an average legionnaire—but not a superbly trained fighter like The Sicillian. Rufus would never allow any mere gladiator to best him in a fight. Now the fight was on and each man fought to the death while hot sparks flung from the loud crashing blades.

There was blood spilled, so far just minor cuts and slashes, at first. As yet neither man had achieved a damaging, or killing blow. And The Sicillian was sure that Mardus had been hired to do just that—to kill him. An assassin—and here in the King's palace! What in all Hades was going on out here in Armenia and the East? The Roman was determined to find out.

"Who hired you, Mardus?" The Sicillian barked at his attacker. The Roman did not want to kill this man if he could help it. He wanted information from his attacker—information which was more important to him now than taking the man's life.

"Would not you like to know that, my bold Roman!" Mardus barked back defiantly.

"Then tell me, or I shall kill you before you can launch your next attack upon me."

"I think not. I have been paid too well."

"But you shall never live to spend your blood money."

"It matters little to me, I do it for my wife and children. With you dead, they will be free! Free of Rome and Romans, whether I live today, or I die!" Mardus told the Roman defiantly. Then he renewed his attack with a headlong desperate fury, hoping to take the Roman unawares. It was an attack by sheer force. As if in the arena, but it was not to be. The Sicillian was too wary a warrior to fall for any simple trick. He stood ready for what was to come, ready to blunt any attack. The Sicillian also knew he would learn nothing more out of this man. The man was bound to secrecy. So be it, it would be a fight to the death.

Mardus came at The Sicillian once again in another wild attack worthy of the gladiatorial games in the Coliseum in *Roma* itself. Rufus waited, saw his opening and then parried and lunged with his own short sword. His trust went in and up, deep into the man's vitals and Mardus suddenly froze, a look of intense shock upon his face, and then he fell down to the floor to be surrounded by a steadily growing blood red pool.

The Sicillian disarmed the man and then went down to hold his head up before he expired. He held his blade to the assassin's throat, but the killer just laughed at that threat. He knew he was a dead man and had accepted the fact long ago. He knew he was beyond any danger now, and only death awaited him.

"Talk to me now, Mardus. This is your last chance to make a clear breast of things. Who paid you? Who do you work for?"

Mardus coughed blood, leaking mightily from his deadly wound. A large red pool surrounded him. The Roman knew the man would not last long.

"Are you in with The Liberators? The Parthians?" The Sicillian demanded of the man, for he still remembered that Praetorian officer Milo and his group of 'charming' professional killers who he had fought and killed in Gaul, while on an earlier mission to Hispania months ago. Could this man and his attack be connected with that somehow?

Mardus just laughed mockingly, spewing blood from his lips.

Another thought occurred to the Roman.

"Do you work for the Parthians? That snake of a Parthian prince who hates Rome?" he demanded of the dying man.

Mardus just smiled, coughed more blood and then quickly died.

The Sicillian set the would-be assassin down upon the cold stone flags of the deserted palace hallway. He lay there surrounded by a large pool of blood, much of the blood was now upon the newly clean uniform of The Sicillian.

Suddenly there was a great commotion from the hallway behind him. It was then that a group of the king's soldiers entered the hallway. The Sicillian turned quickly, his blade out and ready for whatever might come at him. It turned out to be Captain Andorus and his palace guard company, and they had Lord Saskra with them.

"Lower your sword, Roman, you are in no danger from us," the guard captain stated carefully.

The Sicillian, lowered his *gladius*, but did not sheath it yet. It was ever ready for instant use. He was learning that Armenia and the East could be a most treacherous place.

"What has happened here?" the Armenian lord demanded, as he looked over the tableau of a very bloody Roman legion officer in full uniform and a man laying dead in a large pool of blood at his feet.

The Sicillian ignored the Lord Saskra's question, but demanded one of his own from him and Captain Andorus. "Who is this man? Do you know him? He just tried to kill me."

Captain Andorus did not say a word, but only looked askance at the Armenian lord.

"His name is Mardus and he is in my employ, Roman," Lord Saskra told him.

"And did you pay him to murder me?"

"Of course not!"

"Of course not? We shall see," The Sicillian mimicked full of skepticism. Having an assassin under his employ could put the Armenian lord at risk of death, but he was a favorite of the King and high in the council of his people, so Roman anger would have to be cooled in dealing with the man. In any case, Lord Saskra might even be telling the truth, and perhaps he was not involved in the assassination attempt at all.

"We shall see what the King has to say about this matter," Lord Saskra said in an angry voice. He seemed to be genuinely insulted—so either he was a most proficient liar—or he was actually telling the truth. Who could know for sure? The torturers? Perhaps, but that was not going to happen to a high lord so close to the King. Not yet, at any rate.

"Yes, we shall see, my lord," The Sicillian stated as he wiped his bloody sword upon the clothing of the dead Mardus and then sheathed the blade. "I need to see the king immediately."

"Very well," Captain Andorus replied, forming up his men. "We were sent to your chamber to escort you as an honor guard to the feast. When you were not there we set out to find you, Roman. I never thought such a thing like this would happen here, in the palace of the king!"

"Neither did I. Lead, on, Captain."

CHAPTER IV

King Tigranes was much angered and apparently highly insulted when he heard the news of the attempted murder of the emissary of Rome—a messenger from mighty Caesar himself. The fact that Caesar's emissary was almost murdered in his very own palace galled him greatly. Such a thing, had it succeeded would have been a terrible stain upon him and his honor—and his relationship with Rome and with Caesar. It would have been a political disaster. Caesar would never have accepted it. A great punishment would be forthcoming to Armenia and to it's king.

The Sicillian saw all this in the face of the king. At least, it *appeared* that the king was most upset and angered when he learned of the deadly deed. As he should have. The Roman decided that he believed the Armenian king, mostly because his throne was directly balanced on his loyalty to Rome and Caesar Augustus. That was the truth he could not deny and The Sicillian was sure that no king would dare risk his kingdom by such a foolish act—and also risk his life because of it, if it failed. Which it had.

Then the Roman looked over at Lord Saskra and that man seemed to be a different matter altogether. Loyal to his own king—for certain—or possibly—but to Rome? That was a different question. Lord Saskra was a question himself and The Sicillian did not like such questions with unknown answers. His old friend and mentor, the Greek Apollodorus, would never trust such a fellow, so The Sicillian watched the Armenian lord most carefully. Was he, in fact, loyal to the enemy? Loyal to Parthia?

The Parthian, King Phraates IV was a wily old dog. He had been around a long time, knew much, had learned much. He would use diplomacy if it would get him what he wanted. Or assassins if need be. Rufus knew that General Agrippa had the Parthian king hard pressed with his legions on the western Parthian border here in Armenia. Meanwhile, Tiberius had his Roman legions further pressed the Parthians in the north in Syria. So Phraates was feeling severe Roman pressure. It was also rumored that the Parthians were feeling pressure from other peoples far off in their own provinces further in the East.

Then there was Caesar Augustus—and what only The Sicillian knew that the master of Rome's plans were to come here personally with still more legions. Caesar had told only Rufus what his plans were in this regard, and they were bold and cunning—but…?

The Sicillian stood before Tigranes, King of the Armenians and Lord Saskra, as well as Captain Andorus and his palace guard, whose men stood at his side with his men in front of the king's throne. Other royal lords and ladies stood back, quietly looking on in curious fascination. Not one of them muttering a word.

"This is most serious, a great affront to my majesty and to that of Rome," the King began sharply. He was angry and showed it. "An assassination attempt against a messenger from Caesar, in my very own palace!"

"Caesar Augustus will not be pleased when he hears news of this," The Sicillian spoke up, deciding to use his harsh words to put a bit more oil on the fire and see where it burned. And who it might burn.

Lord Saskra seemed to bristle especially at the words, and the cold look he received from the king.

"So be it," King Tigranes proclaimed. "I want everyone associated with this traitor Mardus rounded up and… questioned."

The way he said it, was quite clear, he meant torture. The Sicillian felt sad for the poor man's family and friends, who were all undoubtedly innocent of the plot, but Mardus had set his own ship afloat by his action of treachery and murder—and sunk that ship. That ship of his and all associated with him as well. Unfortunately he had sunk their own lives now, instead of saved them. Such was the penalty for disloyalty—or failure. The tortures would be bad and probably elicit no meaningful information from these sad innocent people who knew nothing. The man to torture for what he knew was Mardus—but he was now dead and so beyond all questioning in any manner.

"But what of Caesar? And Agrippa?" one of the king's nobles finally asked nervously.

"Then let him come, if he must," King Tigranes spoke up with a heavy sigh as he had an aid whisper something in his ear. He nodded thoughtfully, looked up, "He is here now. He has arrived, so there is no sense in holding him up."

The Sicillian looked up at the King and Lord Saskra, then at Captain Andorus, wondering just what the monarch had meant by his cryptic words, but he did not have long to wait to find out.

There was the blaring of legionary trumpets accompanied by the pounding of field drums, and the footsteps of hobnailed legionary boots upon the finely polished stone flags of the palace floor. Suddenly the throne room doors were flung open and in marched Marcus Vipsarius Agrippa, General of the eastern legions of Rome, and the right arm of Caesar Augustus. Behind him were a cadre of hard legionary fighters proudly carrying their eagles and standards.

Agrippa looked as tough and vibrant as ever, sharp of gaze as always, steady and firm. He marched in with his men like the conqueror he was. He was a master strategist and a victorious general who had never known defeat—and he was dearly loyal to Caesar Augustus.

"Sicillian!" Agrippa acknowledged as he walked past Rufus, who was standing in front of the king's throne. "I see our *Princeps* has sent you here on some errand. I hope that it does not interfere or conflict with my own mission for him."

"I am sure that it does not," The Sicillian told Agrippa in a most diplomatic response. In reality both men knew they were different parts of the same mission.

Agrippa just smiled, nodded and then continued forward with his men towards the throne of the Armenian king.

"King Tigranes," Agrippa acknowledged with the very slightest of bows, showing the very slightest of respect, but respect nonetheless. After all, it was he who had put Tigranes upon this throne—and had kept him there!

"Welcome to Armenia, General Agrippa," the king spoke up in a formal but rather friendly manner. The two leaders did get along—they had an understanding.

"Welcome? I and my legions have been quartered in your nation for the last year, and all I hear is 'welcome?'" Agrippa told him with a slight grimace.

"Well, then, General, welcome here to my home, the imperial palace," the king told him allowing a sly grin.

Agrippa nodded, but held back any biting words. If Tigranes was so friendly why had he never invited the general to his palace during the last year? It seemed odd, and somewhat insulting, but he knew the true reason. The king wanted to maintain his seemingly air of independence from Rome—at least as much as possible. It was a good strategy and the general understood strategy. So he accepted it. In any case, Agrippa was here for Caesar, not his own ends, so he kept quite for the moment on that slight.

"Captain Andorus, see to the General's men, and to all his wants and needs," the king ordered in a serious tone. Now that Agrippa was here, the king wanted to make sure he and his men were well taken care of and not prone to causing any mischief.

"Yes, My King," Andorus replied sharply and gave the proper orders to the household staff, who ordered the slaves.

"And now, My General, what it is that is so important that you must take the long and dangerous journey personally from your headquarters all the way out here to my humble palace?"

"What indeed? We need to talk. Privately," Agrippa stated rather abruptly. He could be a most impatient man when he had a mission to perform.

The king nodded, ordered in a loud voice, "Everyone, leave the room at once!"

Captain Andorus and the Romans who had come with Agrippa also now quickly left the room. Lord Saskra stayed. The Sicillian moved off, as if to leave.

"No, he stays, the Sicillian stays," Agrippa ordered, then he looked over at Lord Saskra, "but that one must leave."

"So be it," the king agreed and he gave the order as Agrippa had requested.

"In a moment the great throne room was almost empty. No servants, no slaves, no guards, no court, only the King of Armenia, the General from Rome, and The Sicillian. The three men gathered together in an alcove around a large ornate table. Upon the table was a map of Armenia, Parthia and the eastern regions bordering the Empire of Rome.

"We have a problem," Agrippa spoke up first in a firm tone. He was obviously annoyed and impatient. "We have had a problem since the days of Crassus and Antony many years ago. You understand?"

"Parthia," the king acknowledged with a sagely nod of his regal head.

"Yes, forever Parthia," Agrippa stated with a growl. Then he clapped his hands loudly. "We have one other who will join us now. We have a newly arrived emissary from Caesar, who will now report to us."

Then the doors to the throne room were opened by Roman soldiers and an older distinguished gentleman in red Spartan Greek war cloak and tunic entered the room. It was the wily old Greek, Apollodorus who now entered the chamber. The huge doors of the room were quickly sealed behind him by the Roman guards. The Greek was dressed in the blood red uniform and cloak of a warrior from Sparta—which The Sicillian knew he affected upon occasion when it suited his needs—and he held a large shiny brass 'V' shield and long javelin. He looked the perfect military man, but he was also a noteworthy scholar and teacher.

"Honored Gentlemen," Apollodorus spoke up in a most respectful and mild manner. "General Agrippa, King Tigranes, and my young friend, Rufus. It is good to see you all again, and all here in one place."

"Where else would we be, Greek?" Agrippa growled impatiently, but he was eager to hear what this man had to tell them who had lately arrived from Caesar.

"And where is the Lord Saskra?" the Greek asked thoughtfully.

"I sent him away," Agrippa stated grimly. It was obvious that he did not trust the Armenian lord. The Sicillian allowed a slight nod of his head, he did not trust Lord Saskra either, but that did not bother him now. The man's absence from this meeting did. He knew he would have to remedy that immediately.

"Nonsense, he must be present in any such discussion. Please see to it that he attends us immediately, we have much to discuss at this meeting. I come straight from Caesar Augustus himself with his words that you must hear straight from my lips. All of you, including the Lord Saskra."

General Agrippa shook his head but remained quiet. He knew the wily Greek was as close to mighty Caesar as was he, or The Sicillian.

The Sicillian looked closely at his Greek friend and mentor and hoped the man knew what he was doing. He usually did know what he was doing, so Rufus said not a word. He would be patient and see what happened next.

Lord Saskra was called and when he attended the meeting all was in readiness for what Apollodorus was to tell the four men who were now present. The Sicillian tried to get the eye of his old friend and mentor but the Greek was being as inscrutable and quiet as ever when upon some obvious secret mission. It seemed Caesar had more irons in the fire than just he and the General on this matter.

"Well now, then this is good, we are all here. King Tigranes of Armenia, General Agrippa of Rome, Lord Saskra of Armenia, and my young friend The Sicillian, Rufus," Apollodorus explained, he had put down his shield and javelin—they seemed more for show at this point—and he had taken off his heavy red wool war cloak and now sat at a table with a large goblet of wine. He poured wine for each of the other four men seated at that table. That was the table with the large map of the eastern borders of the Empire, Armenia, and Parthia upon it.

"It is good we are all here now, for we have much to discuss," the Greek began in a low friendly tone. "I come straight from Caesar Augustus with orders for each of you—orders that you may not deny. First off, concerning the man who is not here. Tiberius, while not here, he will also be informed of his part to play in our coming action."

"And what is that?" Agrippa asked boldly, but curious. "Caesar has left me here to grapple with this problem. I have done my best, now I hope that we can be released to go to war and complete the mission. Defeat—and then destroy—Parthia."

"General Agrippa, the Great Augustus applauds your hard work out here on the borders of the Empire and now asks one more action from you—as he does of all of you men here."

Each man looked at the Greek expectantly, waiting for the words from Caesar.

The wily Greek looked from face to face, from king to general, and all acknowledged with a curt nod that they would do whatever Great Caesar asked of them. Did any of them have a choice? Did any of them disagree? Surely not.

"Then it is settled. These are Caesar's wishes as relayed by myself from him, to be obeyed by all," the Greek spoke up in a firm tone. "General Agrippa will ready his legions to attack from Armenia into Parthia—but only upon further word from Caesar. Lord Saskra will lead the Armenian soldiers of King Tigranes against Parthia, under the direction of General Agrippa."

Lord Saskra looked towards his king, who simply nodded in agreement.

Lord Saskra simply bowed his head.

"General Tiberius is presently in Syria with his legions and at the appointed time Agrippa and his Romans—with our Armenian allies under Lord Saskra will invade western Parthia. Tiberius and his army shall invade the northern lands of the enemy."

"Well, it is about time!" Agrippa stated with evident pleasure.

"Then it is war?" King Tigranes asked solemnly.

"It is war," Apollodorus acknowledged rather sadly.

The men there each let that knowledge sink into their thoughts, each according to his own desires. They knew what it meant. The last time Rome had gone to war with Parthia things had not turned out well at all. The legions of Crassus and Antony had lost their invasions in devastating defeats. Worse yet, legionary eagles and standards had been captured and Roman legionaries had been taken prisoner—some of whom were still being held as prisoners—some still held for as much as 30 years later. Crassus himself, had been captured and killed in a gruesome spectacle when he was forced to drink molten gold. Both Roman incursions into Parthia, though taking place in different decades, had been disasters. Now Caesar was planning another invasion of Parthia—and another war—this time to win. For victory or death!

Agrippa was eager as ever; the Armenian king was not, but he was accepting of his place as a ruler of a Roman client state. Lord Saskra seemed most interested. The Sicillian was perplexed and had a dozen questions for his Greek friend—but he dared not voice any of them yet. Not here, certainly not among these other three men.

"There is more, my friends," Apollodorus spoke up with a grim smile. "What no one knows, and what must never leave this room, is that mighty Caesar himself is on his way here with his own legions. No one must know of this. At the time that Agrippa and Tiberius begin their attacks, Caesar's army will strike upwards into Parthia from the south, into the soft underbelly of the enemy's lands. His force shall cut the enemy army off from Agrippa, and Agrippa shall proceed to the capital city and capture King Phraates and his son, that troublesome young prince, Tiridates. That is the rest of the plan, gentlemen, and knowledge of it must never leave this room. You are to prepare your forces immediately, and await further instructions from Caesar—which will be forthcoming."

Agrippa nodded, "Finally! And Caesar shall join the fight! That is all to the good!"

"And what about me and my mission?" The Sicillian asked curiously.

Apollodorus looked at his young friend and simply smiled, "Sorry, my son, you were sent here to see if some diplomatic solution to the return of the eagles and standards was possible. I am afraid that with Prince Tiridates of Parthia, that is not possible."

"There have already been two attempts on my life because of it," Rufus told his friend. He was rather wedded to the idea of his mission because of it.

"Yes, that is too bad, but I see that you are alive and appear none the worse for wear," The Greek smiled at his old friend with an odd glint in his eye that indicated that there was more to this all than he was saying at the moment. "But all that is over now. Your old mission has ended. Tomorrow you and I return to the headquarters camp of Caesar for further orders. And that is the end of that."

The Sicillian only nodded, disappointed that his mission, which had barely started, seemed all but over now. But he decided to say nothing more on the subject until he had some time to talk to the Greek alone and in private.

"King Tigranes, General Agrippa, Lord Saskra, I know that you all have much preparations to make and so I wish you all good hunting. I, and this young whelp, will leave you now and soon make our way back to Caesar's encampment. You are all clear on your parts to be played in the upcoming action?"

"Yes," the Armenian King spoke up.

Lord Saskra nodded thoughtfully. The Sicillian wondered what thoughts were going on in that man's cunning mind.

"Of course," Agrippa stated casually, ready and willing—and waiting.

"Caesar and his legions are on the way, no news of his coming must escape this room upon pain of instant death, you are all to prepare and await his orders. That is all. Is that clear?"

The three men nodded.

"Then I and Rufus shall take our leave of you now. To victory or death!"

CHAPTER V

Once in a secluded suite that had been made available for them in the palace, The Sicillian went out alone upon the terrace overlooking the palace grounds to get some air and clear his head. He was surprised to note a rider quickly leaving the palace—not a Roman either—but a man riding at a furious pace. Towards the East.

Apollodorus saw his young protégé out alone upon the terrace and soon joined him.

"A lonely night, is it not?" the Greek said with a kindly smile, noting the rider now far away.

"An interesting one, at any rate," his young friend replied.

Noting that no one was about, and in a low tone closely spoken, the Greek then said, "Much has changed my friend, has it not?"

"Yes," The Sicillian said, unable to hide his disappointment, and his many questions. He knew The Greek would answer them in his own time, so he did not ask them all straightaway.

"You wanted a chance to try diplomacy so you could get the eagles and standards returned to us?"

"Yes, or at least to try it, before things led to war."

Laudable, I am sure. Well, things have changed, and it is war now for sure."

"Yes, I imagine that it will be."

"You seem sad."

"What will be, will be."

Apollodorus allowed a broad smile, and The Sicillian looked at the man most carefully. Something was certainly up!

"What is it that you and Caesar have cooked up?" he asked his old friend curiously.

"Well, I would be remiss if I admitted there is more to all this than there appears."

"I saw a rider just now leave the palace grounds, he was not a Roman and he was pushing his mount with all haste, very quickly."

"And was he riding towards the East, towards where Parthia lay?" The Greek asked with a wily grin.

"Yes he was."

"Good."

"Good?" The Sicillian asked in an incredulous tone.

"Yes, that is good," his Greek friend replied with a wry grin. "Now I will tell you the rest of the plan."

The Sicillian looked carefully at his Greek friend and mentor awaiting what was to come and knowing it would be something unexpected, daring, and probably very dangerous.

Apollodorus smiled grimly, "There is much activity that will be coming up here in the East, my friend. Much planning set afoot by Caesar that he wants to be put into operation exactly as he wishes. It shall be done just so. There is no alternative."

"So this war…?" Rufus asked ever curious, but wondering.

"Oh, the war is real—or could be—or perhaps it is not? Who can get into the head of Caesar to truly know the truth of his thoughts. But I tell you one thing for certain, he and his legions are surely on the way here. And they are ready for war. And now, apparently—or very soon, or as soon as that rider you saw reaches King Phraates with his news—the Parthians shall know our war plan as well. And they shall know that Caesar himself is on his way to the East."

The Sicillian showed his astonishment at this revelation.

"But why? You gave up secret information about the movement of Caesar! You allowed Lord Saskra to hear our plans and even be a part of them? I never trusted him," Rufus said with obvious annoyance and concern. "And there is more you do not know yet. It was a man named Mardus, who tried to murder me here in this very palace last night—he is certainly one of Lord Saskra's men."

"Yes, I am sure of it," Apollodorus admitted readily.

"You are sure of it?"

"I hope so, certainly."

"So what of this Lord Saskra?"

"Well, it appears the noble lord serves two masters…"

"Or mayhap just one—in Parthia?" The Sicillian replied grimly.

The Greek allowed a sly smile but The Sicillian just shook his head with dismay.

"Perhaps he is in bed with the Parthians? At least I—we, Caesar and I—hope that is the case. We believe it to be true. Regardless, the news that Caesar and his legions are on the way here to begin the invasion will soon be known by the Parthians. That is what Caesar wants.

Then it will be up to the Parthians to act. Now my friend," and the Greek looked at The Sicillian with a grim twisted smile, "before that happens, you and I must make our way to Parthia and seek an audience with King Phraates."

"Truly?"

"Yes."

"When?"

"Now. In fact, we leave immediately."

"Immediately?"

"Yes, I have a change of clothing for us both, pack horses with provisions are set and ready, we can disrobe and bundle our uniforms and weapons. I have other clothing for us that is more appropriate for travel here in the East. Now make ready, we leave before dawn, and we shall be gone before anyone here is the wiser."

The Sicillian nodded and he and the Greek made ready to leave.

CHAPTER VI

It was at that very moment that the Captain of the Palace Guard, Andorus, suddenly entered the suite of the Greek and The Sicillian.

"General Agrippa asks that you come to him immediately, Sicillian."

"Now?"

"Right now! I am to escort you. Come!"

The Sicillian nodded and he and the Greek made ready to follow the captain and his men.

The captain held back Apollodorus, "Greek, the General expressly told me that *you* not be invited to this meeting. Only The Sicillian."

The Greek shrugged, accepting the rebuke in good stead for the moment.

"Go see him Rufus. See what is on his mind. I shall await your return here."

The Sicillian, still wearing his Roman tunic, nodded and then followed the Armenian captain and his men out of the suite.

The Sicillian found General Marcus Vipsanius Agrippa alone in a richly appointed suite of rooms within an entire wing of the palace that he and his men had taken over. Tough tested Roman legionaries stood guard at the door in the outside hall, but no one else was in the room with the general and his visitor.

"Come in, make yourself comfortable," the General told his young guest in an expressive manner. "It has been a few years."

"Yes, it has, General," The Sicillian responded formally wondering what the man wanted from him. Information, most likely. Information he was most probably not willing to be forthcoming with.

"Marcus, please," the General said with a nod of his head. "And I shall call you Gaetano. Like we are old friends met again after some years. That is true, is it not?"

"All right," The Sicillian responded in a friendly manner he did not truly feel.

"So what are you doing here? What mission has Caesar put you upon?"

The Sicillian smiled, he could not really answer that question, and he was sure that the General knew that as well.

"Nothing other than what you have heard," Rufus replied a bit coyly.

Agrippa smiled just as coyly, for he understood all too well the game that was played out these days. "You know why I did not ask that wily Greek to come here with you?"

"You do not like Apollodrus. You have never liked him," Rufus stated boldly.

"Of course not, no you are very much mistaken," Agrippa told him with a sly grin, as if lauding the fact that he knew something Rufus did not. "I bear no animus against the Greek at all, in fact he is a most able man. Actually I like him quite a lot—but I do not *trust* him."

"I see," The Sicillian answered carefully. Curious at this admission by the General, but there was more.

"I am afraid that you do not understand, young Gaetano Rufus," Agrippa told him boldly. "You see I do not dislike the Greek, in fact I rather like him, but I do not *trust* him at all—so he is not invited here. He will never be truthful with me, it is not in his nature to do so. That is the way things are between him and I. Perhaps we are too much alike? I hope not. On the other hand, while I *like* him, I do *not* like you, Gaetano Rufus—but I do *trust* you. So I put my personal feelings aside now to speak with you. You have the trust of Caesar which speaks well of you and is all I need to know. And you are a true Roman. We Romans must stick together."

Rufus hardly knew what to say by this rather stunning and open admission by the general, he nodded most sagely as Apollodorous had taught him to do in such prickly situations. Such political, diplomatic, or sensitive areas of activity that could get a man killed before he ever knew what had happened—or why!

"What are your plans now?" Agrippa asked bluntly.

The Sicillian shrugged, no sense not being forthcoming, it was no military secret. "The Greek and I are ordered to leave here in the morning to report back to Caesar's headquarters and army camp. Beyond that, I know nothing more."

"And what if Apollodorous knows what is to come after…?"

"He has not yet told me," Rufus replied truthfully.

"Hah! That I can well believe, that Greek is a most tricky devil. Do not trust him overmuch. Not one to show his plans until the last moment, have a care with him, young Rufus."

"He has always been true to me."

"Be that as it may, he will be the death of you some day."

"Perhaps," The Sicillian admitted wryly, "but we all must die some time and Hades saves a spot for each one of us when our time here is done."

"Ah, yes, you are right, of course on that score," Agrippa said with a light laugh. He had to admit that he was somewhat amused by this young Roman.

Rufus had stated his words rather grandly, but knowing the Greek as he did he could well see that Agrippa might be right. Who knew what the future held, and who could tell what way the winds might blow concerning the whims of Caesar and Imperial Rome?

Agrippa stated simply, "We have a mission for Caesar and Rome before us out here in the East. War is coming. I am happy that Caesar has given his imprimatur to the coming conflict between the Empire and Parthia. It has been too long in the coming. Overdue, in fact."

"Yes, it is, as the Greeks often say, something that is inevitable," Rufus replied in agreement with the General.

Agrippa nodded. "I *trust* you, Sicillian, but I do not *like* you. You know why?"

"I am a friend to Caesar and he uses me as he will to do his bidding and to extend the Empire. His Empire?"

"No, not at all, he uses us all in that manner. I do not like you because you are such a true believer in the man. That is dangerous for you—and perhaps for us all. Maybe even Caesar himself."

"But you are just as loyal and true to him. Maybe even more so than I!"

"Yes, and I shall continue to be loyal to Caesar until my death, but you are something different, you worship him as an older brother, or father. Or dare I say it, a god? He is not. He is just a man. With faults."

"Very few of them."

"That may be true."

"He is good for Rome," The Sicillian added with a sureness he truly felt.

"He has ended the republic," Agrippa answered with a tinge of sadness that had crept into his voice.

Rufus looked at the General in a new light now, and with a sharp gaze. Was he a secret Liberator? It certainly appeared he had let his vail slip and shown that he had such sympathies. Could it be possible? Never! Or so he hoped…

"That is strange talk coming from one so loyal, as Marcus Vipsanius Agrippa," The Sicillian told the general.

"I see the writing on the wall as plain as day and in the light of day, young fellow. You, I am afraid, do not," Agrippa told him in a blunt tone. "It is sad, Rome has fallen into dictatorship, and does not even know it, and Great Caesar Augustus is the worst harbinger of that—and all the evil that shall come from it after he is gone."

"How can you say that? You are a loyal friend and serve him well. You have helped place him in his position as ruler—and keep him there! You have seen how well he rules, the peace and stability he has brought after years of civil war and strife. Caesar Augustus is the best thing that has happened to Rome since—Romulus and Remus!"

Agrippa just laughed.

The Sicillian grew angry and showed it.

"Oh, fear not, Rufus, I am not mocking you, but the situation. However, think on this. Caesar Augustus by being such a great, and even perfect emperor, of which he truly is—I do not doubt that for one moment—has opened the door to that pattern of rule for Rome henceforth. That is not a good thing. For just as Augustus has proved to be a great man—who knows what type of man—or beast—will succeed him? Someone drunk on ultimate power! The republic is dead, we will now be ruled by emperors with absolute power. Absolute power for good—or evil. Augustus is fair and very competent, but what of the others that follow him? Remember, I know something of the vile snakes that inhabit the Senate in Rome. I fear for Rome—in the future and I fear those emperors that shall follow Augustus. Not the wise ones—few as they may be—but the bloody ones, the fools, the incompetents—and the monsters. None shall be able to fill the boots of Augustus, yet all shall have the great power of Caesar Augustus to do with as they will. That is my great fear, my friend."

The Sicillian nodded deeply, much of what Agrippa said made sense, even though he did not like to hear it. The man truly was a strategic thinker whose mind ranged far ahead and into realms of thought most people never even imagined.

"But I ramble on, my friend, do not concern yourself with my own small worries."

"I think I see what you mean, General," Rufus stated, for he had often had similar thoughts upon the matter—upon the future of Rome—after Augustus. "But what good can we do about it? The future, as Apollodorous has told me many times, is unwritten. Unknowable. It is always amenable to change by the hands of man. Or men. So your worst fears may not ever come to be."

"So it is, perhaps," Agrippa agreed with a slight smile. "I just wanted to have this chance to speak to you before the war begins. It shall be a long and bloody war—Rome shall win—I shall guarantee that—for we can not afford to lose again against Parthia—but the cost will be truly great."

"Caesar wants those eagles and standards returned," The Sicillian told the General. "That is all he desires. That is what he really wants."

"Yes, of course, and so he tells us all, but do you believe that that is what this war is truly about? I see more to it. It is about extending his domains, expanding the Empire here in the East—and punishing Parthia. All ideas that I fervently agree with, by the way."

"Then we shall see," The Sicillian spoke up calmly. "We each have our duty to Rome and Caesar, General. I have answered your questions to the best of my ability and now I must be gone."

"Then good luck to you, young Gaetano, in whatever path you take."

"And to you too, General."

The Sicillian left the General as soon as he could do so, eager to get back to his chambers and find out what his companion knew about what was to come.

CHAPTER VII

"Well? What did he say? What did he want?" was the first thing Apollodorous asked him when The Sicillian returned to their suite of rooms at the other end of the palace.

Rufus told his companion some of the conversation he'd had with the General, but not all of it.

"Well, he seems a most complex man, and dare I say it, a great man," the Greek stated thoughtfully. He knew Rufus was holding back on some of the conversation with the General. It was only natural.

The Greek continued, "Well, then, to other matters at hand now. I have been busy while you have been gone. I have civilian clothing here for us. We must change into them straight away. I also have pack horses supplied and ready. We leave immediately for the capitol of King Phraates IV of Parthia. May the gods preserve us!"

The Sicillian and the Greek leading a pack horse each, and with two additional remounts each, secretly left the palace of the King of Armenia and sped eastward.

So far the Fates had been with them, they had not been challenged leaving the palace—no one was ever challenged *leaving* the palace, only *entering* the palace—nor had they been challenged leaving the city. It was odd, but this was Armenia, and the far East, not *Italia* and Rome. Things were done differently out here. More lax, less serious. It was an older world here, and the people did not overly concern themselves with what was—and what would be. They had a stoic acceptance of all situations. Not like the Romans at all, who never accepted anything they did not agree with, and always worked to change what they did not like. But Rome was Rome—and the East was the East.

"We have to move quickly, reach Ctesiphon on the Tigris and somehow get an audience with King Phraates before this war begins," The Greek told his young friend. "Caesar and his legions are already in Judea and he has made his headquarters in Caesarea, ready to march. Tiberius and his legions are in Syria and will move eastward, while Agrippa and the Armenian auxiliaries, will push across from the East. Caesar will strike up into the soft underbelly of Parthia from the south through Judea. I fear the war will go on for years. Perhaps a million dead all told."

The Sicillian nodded ominously at the death toll. That was grim news. Could it be possible? That many dead? Both men said little after that as they pushed their mounts onward to faster speed.

After many hours riding across the broad plains of this border region, the Sicillian spoke up to his companion, "We are being followed."

The Greek nodded firmly, "Yes, they have been with us since we left Armenia, but always hanging back, waiting."

"Waiting for what?"

"Waiting to take us unawares. They have been well prepared, given instructions on how best to take us down, and where to do it," Apollodorus told him. "We shall do the same. I have a few ideas on how to deal with them. Come, let us increase our pace, make them wear out their mounts, for I see they do not have remounts as we do."

"The remounts slow us down," The Sicillian noted, though he was glad to have them.

The Greek nodded, "True, but we will need them. In any matter we will soon meet those who follow us, and have to deal with them out here in the wilds. When they decide to come upon us. We can but be ready for them—and then, by the gods, kill them all."

"Do it quick."

"Quick, but if we can capture one and get some information, that would be best, so keep your eyes open for any opportunity to take a prisoner," the Greek said, then added, "but please try not to get yourself killed doing it."

"I will do my best on that score. I had no idea you cared so much, Apollodorous,' The Sicillian said with a grim laugh.

"Oh, I do not care all that much, but it is a long and lonely road to Ctesiphon and it is always best when on the road to have an agreeable traveling companion for good conversation. That is all."

"Hah, that is all! So I am just good conversation?"

"And if you believe that, young lad, you are a real fool."

"I know that," The Sicillian replied hiding a wan grin.

The Greek smiled softly, allowing rare emotion, "You know I jest, my lad. Merely rough playful banter for the road. In actuality, you are like a son to me—the son I never had—or the one I never knew about, eh?"

"Too many of those, I will wager."

The Greek grinned mischievously, "I'll never tell. Ah now, here is action, here they come! Now look lively, they are moving up on us fast. There is an outcropping of rocks up ahead that would make a perfect place for an ambush and I am sure they seek to lead us to it. A trap that they could box us in, so they can kill us easily. We shall accommodate them by entering their trap, but give them the surprise of their lives once they enter to kill us. Be wary. Here they come!"

There were four of them. They wore no uniforms. Black riders on fast horses. They rode like fury, exhilarated in the fact that they had driven their two prey and their pack horses into a small defile where they could kill them easily and quickly.

It was not to be that easy. Once the attackers reached the defile, The Sicillian and the Greek were already dismounted and waiting for them from above upon the rocks. They dove down upon the first two riders and with their daggers quickly cut the throats of two of the attackers. The two men never knew what hit them, never expecting an attack from above. Now the odds were equal, and that meant it was bad for the attackers.

"What happened?" one of the remaining two attackers shouted out fearfully to his companion. Shocked. Fearful.

"Shut your trap and kill them!" the man responded in anger.

"You'll not take us so easily!" the Greek shouted back as he drew his short Spartan sword.

The Sicillian already had his *gladius* out and ready.

The two remaining riders were shocked that two of their number already lay dead at their feet. The attack upon them had been so quick and brutal, a mere execution worthy of the gladiatorial games they were so familiar with, but quite effective. But it was nothing more than what they had intended for the two Romans.

The Sicillian would come down upon his attacker first, quickly, for he knew the rider could not maneuver his mount in the tight defile, and here they had made a grievous error in their ambush tactics and attack. They were mounted men and found themselves hemmed in by the rocks as well as the horses of their two dead companions, and the pack horses and remounts belonging to the Roman and the Greek. It was quite crowded for any mounted man in that tight defile to maneuver his mount effectively. That was when the two attackers were set upon from above. The Sicillian and the Greek had bounded up the rocks immediately and moved along the defile until they were in a position right above the remaining two approaching riders. Then they struck!

The Sicillian dove down upon his man, knocking him off his horse in a sharp attack. The two fought like furies upon the ground. The Roman used his short sword and dagger effectively blocking off the blows of his enemy. His enemy never knew what hit him, but he was a wily fellow and recovered soon. Then came at the Roman hard. A serious battle raged between them.

"You'll not take me so easily, Roman!" the attacker shouted as if it were a promise. He was a tough burly fellow, deadly and dangerous.

The Sicillian just offered him a grim smile and came at the man all the harder. He took a second to look over at how his companion was doing, and he could see that the Greek was battling the other rider, having him dismounted and hard pressed against a rocky wall of the defile. The man had no place else to go, he was trapped. It was not long before the sword of the Greek found the heart of his enemy. The man fell down with a horrid scream of pain, soon to lay dead in a pool of blood.

"There is only one of them left now—your man," Apollodorous informed Rufus as the young Roman fought hard against his attacker, the lone remaining attacker. "Try not to kill him, we need him for questioning."

"Easier said than done," The Sicillian shouted back, for the two men were in a heated battle, one that could go either way.

"You'll get nothing out of me, Roman!" the remaining attacker spat back defiantly. "I will tell you nothing!"

"Rufus, hold him off, I will be there in a moment and then we can take him down together. We can make him talk—I am sure of it—he is worth more to us alive than dead."

The Sicillian nodded, but his attacker saw the way things were to be soon and moved backwards—but he did not try to get away. Instead, the attacker quickly withdrew a dagger from his belt, and as The Sicillian made himself ready for a throw to come at him, the man did a surprise move by taking the blade of his dagger and running it in a deep slice across his own throat. The blood gushed out in a spurting stream and the man shouted one last message of defiance, "You'll get nothing out of me, Roman!"

Then the last of the four attackers fell down dead in a gory pool of blood, his throat leaking viciously even as The Sicillian tried to save him. Rufus did his best to hold the man's neck wound closed, giving the attacker a few precious seconds of life.

"Talk, tell me know, who paid you? Who do you work for? Why attack us?" Rufus shouted at the man. By this time the Greek had come over and was helping, but it was all to no avail. The man had lost consciousness, and then…

"He's dead, Rufus."

"Yes, but why did he take his own life?"

"He is certainly not the type to do such a thing," the Greek agreed.

"Yes, and that troubles me." Rufus replied, examining the man more closely, his clothing, weapons, looking for any personal objects.

"That is the question and one I fear the answer to," the Greek responded as the two men quickly looked over the bodies and goods of their four attackers for any information or evidence of who they were, or who employed them. As expected, the four were clean of any such material. Professional assassins, not very good ones, for sure, but they were hired killers nonetheless. And the fact that their leader took his own life meant that whoever employed these men had put more fear into them than their own life was worth if they failed in their mission. They had, indeed failed.

"These men were dead already, Rufus," the Greek proposed carefully, thinking what it might mean. "We are up against an enemy who does not fear death—or against an enemy who puts such fear into their hired killers that they would rather take their own life than surrender or talk. That is very troubling."

The Sicillian nodded in agreement. "Who could they be? Who could they work for?"

"That is anyone's guess, my lad."

"Hired out of Armenia?" The Sicillian asked.

"Could be, who knows, my young friend. It disturbs me that this last man, obviously their leader, took his own life rather than surrender to us. He knew we would question him—very hard if need be—so he knew we would get what he knew out of him one way or the other. It bothers me that rather than surrender and give up what he knew, he took his own life. That indicates a depth of dedication, even fanaticism, we have not encountered before. I like it not."

"Neither do I."

"Well, it is all water under the bridge now, let us get our horses and be on our way. We have to get to Ctesiphon as soon as we can do so."

CHAPTER VIII

The murder attempt had failed but The Sicillian and the wily Greek were ever more watchful as they entered Parthian territory and headed towards the lush land between the Tigris and Euphrates Rivers. Once there they made their way to the capitol city of Ctesiphon—where the God King Phraates IV ruled a vast empire as large and powerful as Rome itself. In fact, it was said that between Rome and Parthia, these two empires ruled all the lands that made up the known world.

"It will be a strange country, unlike any you have ever seen before, perhaps unlike anything you have ever imagined, Rufus," Apollodorus told his young friend as they continued their furious ride ever eastwards. "They are a strange breed and the mysterious East holds many mysteries. Weird religions, strange rites and secret societies beyond the ken of Greeks and Romans and other civilized people."

"Haven't you told me that the Parthians are decedents of the Ancient Persians and that they have a culture that goes back many thousands of years—even before Rome—even before Greece?" The Sicillian told his friend, unable to resist a bit of nudging the older Greek's historical sensibilities.

"Ah, yes, well that might be correct," Apollodorous reluctantly agreed, offering an ironic smile, then he quickly added, "but the Romans look at them as barbarians, and so they be so to us as well."

The Sicillian nodded with a slight leer, Parthians or Persians, they were just as deadly. He knew quite well what he and the Greek were getting themselves into, but they were on a secret mission for Caesar Augustus and there was nothing for them to do about it but see it through to whatever end lay in store for them. The Sicillian just accepted that grim fate as he pushed his Batavian steed to a greater pace. Ever eastward! He dared not think of his beloved Octavia, for at this point in time he feared he would never see her again. So he tried not to think of her for now.

Apollodorous and his Sicillian companion rode on through the mysterious lands of Parthia in the East, finally reaching the massive Tigris River and then they came to the trading city of Hatra. Here they decided to stay over for one night. They were exhausted, and so were their mounts. All needed food and rest.

It would prove a most interesting night.

Hatra seemed to be a cesspool of lust and all types of dangers that could prove deadly in so many ways, especially to any unwary traveler. However, it seemed to be an open city. Open to all. That was most curious. There were no guards at the gate, and once the two travelers rode through the main city gate they were greeted by a sight they had never seen before, except in the worse districts of the suburbs in Rome.

"I have never ridden into a city where the whores welcome a man so boldly, so openly!" Apollodorous said as he leered at all the displays of female flesh that were on display seemingly for the taking. But he knew the truth. Make an assignment with one of these tempestuous young lovlies and you would find yourself robbed and beaten and left to die in a dark alley without even a kiss from the gal for compensation.

"I have never seen the likes!" The Sicillian said with a heated whisper.

"It is something to look at, is it not, Rufus."

"Something for sure," The Sicillian said seeing the women of Hatra so opening showing their bodies now turned his thoughts to those few nights with Octavia. He thought of her more now, even as he looked at some of the more passionate of the city women with open lusts.

"Come here! You are a Roman, are you not?" one of the whores shouted to Rufus.

"You, Greek! I have something to show you!" and that woman boldly lifted up to show what was under the back of her skirt, ample buttocks. "I know the Greek way!"

The Sicillian just laughed and looked at his friend with a knowing nod.

"Ah, not my way," the Greek said to his young Roman friend. "Why does everyone think that just because I am a Greek…"

"Yes, yes, I am sure," Rufus said with another playful laugh as the two men rode further on into Hatra, down a tight avenue accosted all the way by the shouts of bold whores and others who were selling all manner of things to travelers.

"Interesting city," The Sicillian said in a rather cynical and obvious understatement to his companion.

"One believes one can purchase anything at all here," The Greek replied as the two men made their way to what appeared to be a somewhat decent tavern. "Maybe we can stop here for a few hours, get some food, feed the horses, rest our weary bones, then be on our way at dawn."

"That sounds good, but this place you have chosen…"

"What, do you see any place better?"

The Sicillian shrugged, he had to reluctantly agree that he did not.

"This could be a dangerous place, so watch yourself," Apollodorous told his young Sicillian friend.

"Yes, and you as well," Rufus said, and the two men just laughed. They were ever ready for trouble—especially when in the service of Caesar.

They made arrangements with the tavern owner to have their horses looked after, and then ordered food and drink for themselves. The tavern owner went off to get their food and drink and left the two weary travelers at a table they had chosen in the back of the one main room of the place. It was a bit of a pig's sty, no better than most, but better than some. It would do for a few hours.

"This is a good spot, our backs to the wall, so no one can sneak up behind us and do us dirty," Rufus said as he looked around at the tavern's clientele. The place seemed to be nothing less than a den of thieves, and both men realized that while this might have been the best such establishment that they had seen, it was by no means safe.

"You noted the four stout men at the door when we came in? The tavern owner's slaves, especially used to take care of troublesome customers I should guess."

The Sicillian nodded, he had noted the four men. They looked to be ex-gladiators, or just plain former military. Maybe from the legions? Tough and dangerous men. There was no serious trouble in this tavern. At least not yet.

The tavern owner finally came to their table accompanied by two female slaves who carried trays full of dishes with meats and fruits and flagons of the local ale. The women put the food down on the table. The Greek's mouth watered as he looked at the food and also at the young female slaves. Rufus looked at his friend with some disapproval, and the Greek only gave off a slight grin, then sighed as his eyes moved from the charms of the young ladies to the food.

"You said you wanted the best we offer, and you paid for the best, in Roman gold no less, so here it is," the tavern owner said rather expectantly. He had already been paid, so what was he waiting for.

"This is fine, thank you," the Greek told the man.

"Anything else, sirs, with money? A room, a woman—two women!"

"No, nothing else," the Greek responded, even as it pained him to do so. They were on a mission and time was of the essence. "Just make sure our horses are watered and feed, brushed down, and ready to run at dawn."

"So you leave us at dawn?" the man asked.

"I did not say that," Apollodorous replied with an annoyed look. He did not like anyone who asked too many questions.

"A Greek and a Roman traveling together. That raises all kinds of questions here in Parthia, even in a friendly town like Hatra," the man continued in an oily tone.

"Not your concern, tavern man, just do your job, you have been well paid," the Greek said in a more stern voice. He hoped the man would get the hint and leave them be now, but the man seemed insistent on something.

"No trouble, good sirs," the man replied with that oily grin.

"Are our horses being taken care of, or do I need to go and check them?" The Sicillian asked the man, changing the subject.

"They are all fed and ready to go. So you are on your way to Ctesiphon?"

"Why do you say that?" the Greek asked suspiciously, openly annoyed now. The man was asking too many questions and seemed to know a bit too much.

"No, nothing, good sirs, nothing at all. Everyone who comes through Hatra eventually makes their way to Ctesiphon. It is the capital of Parthia and the hub of the empire. You two seem to be…I wonder…"

"You wonder what?" the Greek asked sharply.

"You think too much for a tavern keeper," The Sicillian said in warning. His hand reached for the hilt of his sword, as did the Greek reach for his weapon, and then the place erupted into turmoil and violence as the four head-breakers who worked the front door were suddenly upon them. The four had snuck up on the two travelers, while the tavern keeper had distracted the two travelers, now the four had somehow came out from a hidden door that opened behind their table.

"Damn Hades! A secret door behind us!" The Greek warned loudly as he and The Sicillian jumped up from their seats and fought off the four attackers. The four thugs came at the travelers with studded clubs and knives. They held no swords or daggers. It was apparent they were not out to kill the two travelers, but to capture them. Probably to sell them as slaves, or to sell them to that Parthian prince who hated Romans so much.

The Sicillian evaded two of the men who were coming for him and was able to catch the tavern keeper and grasp him in his arms with his dagger to the man's throat. "Call your men off, or I slit your throat from ear to ear."

The tavern keeper screamed, then shouted out to his four thugs to back off.

The four thugs stopped their attack and moved slowly back.

"That was wise," The Sicillian said as he continued to hold the tavern owner hostage. Then he and the Greek quickly packed some of their food and drink and then made their way out of the tavern. Rufus still held the tavern keeper hostage and his men were ordered to back off. The two travelers made their way to the barn at the side of the tavern, and were able to get their horses. All had been fed and watered, in fact they looked quite well taken care of, but then the Greek realized that had they been one minute late, their mounts would have been sold to the fat Persian who was already there with a bag of coins to buy all of their horses. It was not to be.

"You'll not get these horses, my fat Persian friend," Apollodorous said, then he grabbed the Persian's small sack and hefted it to hear the joggling of the coins within. Gold? Silver? It did not matter, the man was going to buy their horses after he and his companion had been sold into slavery, or worse, sold to the mad prince. Or just murdered outright. That was not to be.

"Not the proper way to treat travelers to your fine city!" The Sicillian told the tavern keeper as they mounted their warhorses, while the Greek took the reins of their other horses. "Get up!"

"What?"

"You are coming with us to ensure no one comes after us. If you behave and we are allowed to get away from here, we will leave you outside the city wall unharmed," The Sicillian said calmly. Then he looked at the man meaningfully, "Or I can just kill you now!"

"No!"

"Then tell your men, and the people here in the street to stay away and allow us leave unmolested."

"You heard the Roman! Do not interfere with him and the Greek! I order you, upon pain of death, as the agent of the Prince of Parthia!"

The people made to obey and Rufus looked at his Greek friend in evident surprise.

"Had I known that, Rufus, I would never have given him the chance to live, but we made a promise to him, and we shall keep it."

The Sicillian nodded, "You are a lucky man, even for a crooked sniveling worm who works for the mad prince.

The two travelers left the tavern man safely outside the city wall as they had promised, and the man smiled back at his captors as he was let go.

"You should smile, you are alive, but do not send your men after us," the Greek warned the man.

"No, there is no need now for me to do so. You are headed towards Ctesiphon, so the prince will take care of you both. He is already awaiting your arrival."

The Greek looked at his companion, "Not good, my friend."

"I know.

"Come on, let us get out of here!"

The two rode off with all haste and were not followed at all. They did not know if they were happy about that, or if it gave them an ominous feeling. Where they were going, who could tell.

From Hatra the two travelers continued their journey East without interruption until they reached the Parthian capital city of Ctesiphon, where King Praates IV ruled his vast empire. Ctesiphon proved to be a large walled city, much like Rome, built upon the mighty Tigris River. It was quite impressive and as they approached it the two men were very much in awe of the city. It was magnificent. It was the seat of a great empire that rivaled Rome itself.

"What do we seek here?" The Sicillian asked the older man who rode alongside him as they pushed their mounts ever forward towards the city gate.

Finally his companion answered the question he had asked many times before.

"That is a good question. We seek the Parthian, Lord Xenophon, who I am told is a Roman agent," Apollodorous told his young companion as they crossed the mighty Tigris on a bridge manned by elite

Parthian troops. These were not the conscripts seen through most of the country, but professional soldiers. Grim and tough.

The Greek showed the officer in charge a special medallion that bore the likeness of King Phraates on it, and at the same time handed the man a small bag that jingled with the sound of gold or silver coins. The same bag he had taken from the Persian horse buyer the night before. The officer was suitably impressed with the payment and let the two newcomers pass over the bridge unmolested. The officer gave the Greek back the medallion of the king—but kept the bag of jiggling coins.

"Bribes, and they work in the king's own city," The Sicillian said.

"Such is the manner of things here in the East and especially Parthia, Rufus," Apollodorous told his friend as the two rode across the large stone bridge and into the valley between the two rivers—the fertile and rich land that was the heart of Parthia.

"Ctesiphon is not far from here, you can see it plainly at the center of the valley" the Greek informed his companion, "and once there we must immediately seek out Lord Xenophon."

"And who might he be?" The Sicillian asked ever curious now that his companion was suddenly being more forthcoming with information.

"An agent of Caesar and Rome who is in the Parthian camp. As you have no doubt already guessed," Apollodorous told him grimly, then he shrugged. "Or so I was told by Caesar. A spy, or a fellow traveler. At the time Caesar did not seem so certain of the loyalty to Rome of this vaulted Lord Xenophon, but we have no choice but to seek him out to get his aid now. Still, we must tread lightly once we enter the capital."

"I see, so I get the feeling that this Lord Xenophon is either an agent *of* Rome—or an agent *against* Rome? Either he will help us—or he will sell us out?" the youth asked the older man a bit testily. He knew the way politics worked. This seemed like a plan spawned in Hades for sure. He hated all the duplicity.

"Rather indelicately put, but essentially correct. Rome does not have much leverage out here in the far eastern realms, and has many enemies," the Greek explained as they rode down a busy roadway filled with caravans and wagons of various merchants and slavers, among them were many people dressed in the eastern fashion who seemed to be travelers and traders. Maybe some of them even were!

"So we are up to our neck in trouble with no way to go but on-ward?"

"Yes, we will seek out this Lord Xenephon and, for good or ill, we will then see where our mission will lead us. To success or failure, but after all, we all must die some time, eh, Rufus?"

The Sicillian simply nodded, accepting the hard pragmatism of the older Greek's words. "So be it then. I would just like to have it come later, rather than sooner. In any case, we will seek out this Parthian lord and see if he can get us into the palace to have a private audience with the king. That should not be such a problem for a powerful lord."

"Yes, you would think not, but…"

"But what?" The Sicillian asked dubiously, wondering if there was more that his companion was not telling him about this mission.

"Who can say anything for certain in these difficult times. The Par-thian lord is said to be friendly to Rome and also much loved by King Phraates, but not much loved at all by the King's son, Prince Tiridates, who is said to be a most dangerous man, rather unstable, and a fel-low who hates Rome and all things Roman," Apollodorous informed Rufus, adding fuel to the fire in his own imitable manner, then adding, "Including us, no doubt!"

"Well that is certainly interesting to hear at this late hour. When were you going to tell me all this?"

"I just did!"

"I do not mean that! I mean, why did you not tell me sooner?"

"I was to tell you when you had a need to know."

"So I have a need to know, now?"

"Yes, I believe so," the wily Greek said with a twisted grin, fol-lowed by a dry chuckle.

"Thank you," The Sicillian growled cynically, "and is there any-thing else you have neglected to tell me about this mission?"

"I do not believe so, but I am sure you will think of something."

The Sicillian shook his head in exasperation.

"Oh, come now, Rufus, you know how things must be—should one—or both of us be taken captive and tortured for what we know… The least you know, the…better…"

"So you were just protecting me then?" The Sicillian said even more exasperated now.

"And the mission."

"Yes, the mission."

"Ah, well, yes, I think that about sums it up."

"I see," The Sicillian replied rather tight-lipped, holding down his Roman anger. While he was indeed angry, he was more angry because he knew that his Greek friend was probably correct. That irked him more than the fact that certain key information on this mission had been kept from him by his friend and mentor.

"Rufus, you know I am right."

"Come on," The Sicillian growled, "let us ride hard. I can see the city there on the horizon, and if we make haste we may make it within the gates before dusk."

"Yes, that would be wise, they close the city gates at dusk, I am told," the Greek added and the two men rode on quickly.

"Of course they would close the gates at dusk, so let us ride!" and The Sicillian spurred his sleek black Batavian warhorse onward.

CHAPTER IX

As it turned out they made the city and the open gate with time to spare. Both men rode up on their single mounts, for they had left their other horses on the road to get there with all speed, but they still each led a pack horse loaded with the remainder of their food and trade goods, and with their Roman uniforms and arms, which were secretly bundled and hidden. So far they had met with no searches and the offers of the Greek's gold had held off all soldiers who might seek to inquire about their identities and purpose in their coming here and did not search too closely.

"Ctesiphon, Rufus!" Apollodorous told his friend in a bold tone, as though he had a love of the city—or he may have been here before. Had he? He had never admitted as much to Rufus. "You have been here before?"

"What makes you say that?"

"No reason."

The Greek smiled slyly, but volunteered nothing. So The Sicillian took it that his Greek friend had indeed been here before. Probably upon some other secret mission?

The two travelers rode up to the large walled city, up to the still open gate. The city was a gleaming stone habitation of tall buildings and wide streets and sprawling avenues. There were massive temples, minarets and towering ziggurats. It was a quite lovely city, not Roman at all, but exuding wealth and power in the same manner that Rome did. There was a definite Greek flavor to it though, and perhaps an Athenian bent to the architecture of the buildings. No wonder, Rufus thought, that his friend seemed to be entranced by this greatest of Parthian cities.

The two travelers, who now posed themselves as buyers of rare silks and fragrant essences, carefully approached the main gate of the city. The gate was open and many travelers and soldiers were passing through it at a steady pace. No one seemed to be bothered by the guardsmen on duty there. Not yet. And the city guards did not seem to bother anyone coming into the city—or leaving it. Not yet.

The large contingent of armed guardsmen could block the entrance most effectively when they felt it necessary. One of them, who strode with the bearing and arrogance of an officer approached the two travelers from Rome. Behind him were a half dozen armed guardsmen, who looked to be nothing more than ordinary cutthroats. The Sicillian had seen and dealt with their likes before.

"Dismount!" the order was firm.

The two travelers came down off their horses slowly.

The soldiers came closer, surrounding the two men.

"Names, nationality, and state your business!" the soldier, who as surely an officer barked out his command to Apollodorous and The Sicillian impatiently.

The Greek smiled, it was agreed beforehand that he would lead the conversation for the time being. "Worthy sir, my name is Apollodorous, and I am a Greek from Athens. I deal in rare silks and fragrant essences. This one here, is my Roman slave, Rufus, who accompanies me. He is like most Romans, a dull oaf, worthless, but he does his job—or I beat him."

"A large oaf though."

"Yes, but dull witted, stupid, as are most Romans," the Greek replied with a knowing nod at the officers. "Were that all Romans were so dumb-minded."

The guard captain looked closely at the Roman youth, "He certainly looks big enough, he could have been a soldier."

"Hah!" the Greek replied with a wide laugh. "No, not this one, he is just a big, dull farm boy. You know how they all are, they have muscle, but no brain. Just block-headed oafs. Say something, slave!"

The Sicillian tried to hold back his annoyance and merely bowed his head and looked confused. Lowering his eyes.

"See what I mean? A large dullard, but he does his work."

The guards and their captain laughed, taken in completely by the Greek's ruse. Rufus, continued to keep his eyes low, acting the humble slave, but seething with annoyance.

Rufus looked over at the Greek with some surprise, but kept quiet, Dull? Slave? Beaten? He did not show his annoyance, it was not easy for him, then he inwardly laughed, for he realized that the wily Greek had not told him that particular part of his plan, but he knew it was the right thing to say to these soldiers of Parthia. It was the right part for him to play at this time as well.

The truth of it was, a Greek these soldiers could stomach, even as much of this empire had been influenced by things Greek—especially by Alexander The Great—but they could not stomach a Roman—and Rufus was only too obviously a Roman. No, they could not stomach any Roman here unless he was presented to them as a slave. That meant all the difference to them. They liked that turn about of things.

"You have pack horses? What is in the bundles? I see weapons," the officer added curiously, he was glancing at the young Roman and laughing cruelly, the man was not alarmed yet. All travelers carried weapons, if they were wise, and if they could afford them.

"Yes, the weapons are for myself and this worthless slave, a lazy young lout to be sure, but all I can afford these days for my security in my old age as I travel the world to bring wise men like yourself some of the niceties of civilized living. We must protect ourselves from brigands and thieves as best we are able. Brave guardsmen like yourselves I am sure understand that. These are difficult times, my friend."

"I am not your friend," the guard captain shot back with a growl, but he seemed to accept the Greek's story—up to a point. "But I am sure that a trader of your many years must have much success in selling your wares, and being a generous man, you would like to share that success with the hard working soldiers of the king."

Apollodorous did not let a heartbeat skip by as he quickly took out a small purse of jiggling coins, "Of course, my gallant commander. That is why I am proud to present this token of respect to you and your brave men, so you may have a drink on me after your guard shift here is through for the night."

The Greek handed over the small purse of coins to the officer. The purse jiggled with coins, not gold or silver, but they would prove good enough.

"Ah, Greek, you are a wise one, and pass that over here quickly. Me and my men have a powerful thirst and will drink your health later tonight," the officer stated happily, smiling and his men smiled with him. He realized that never was robbery so sweet and so pleasantly agreeable.

"Pass the Greek, and your lowly dull Roman slave. Welcome to Ctesiphon, and if you have need of a friend while here"—and here the officer gave the Greek and leering wink—"or wish to part with any more of your goods, then seek out Captain Tzana and me and my men will always be available to you—for the proper price, of course."

"Of course, my gallant captain, I would expect nothing less," the Greek chimed in.

The Sicillian just looked down at the ground, playing the part of the obedient slave as best he could. It infuriated him, but he realized the ruse and knew it was a good one to play in this city of the enemy.

"Well good captain, there is one tiny service you might aid me with," the Greek asked carefully.

The guard captain frowned, then thought better of it, shrugged and asked, "And what might that be?"

"Can you show me the way to the house of Lord Xenophon?"

The captain looked hard at the Greek, then just laughed, "Lord Xenophon's home is the large palace at the end of this street, but you'll not find him there. The Prince has had him executed. For what reason, I do not know. The Prince executes people for his own personal reasons, best not to inquire too closely, but that lord is dead and gone now."

Apollodorous nodded grimly, hiding his surprise and concern, then looked quickly at Rufus and bade him not speak or show any emotions about this bad news.

"Obviously it was a wise decision by your noble Prince," the Greek said in his most fawning tone.

The guard captain shrugged, uncaring, "Who can say. Pass on now! Pass on!"

Once the two travelers had passed the gate house and the guards, and entered the city proper, they stopped to get their bearings and conferred on what they should do next.

"This appears to be a real problem?" The Sicillian asked his companion, when they had ridden down the broad avenue into Ctesiphon and stopped down the street from the house—or palace—of the lately deceased Lord Xenophon.

"Well, I must admit, this is an unexpected crimp in my plan," the Greek spoke up with some annoyance to his companion.

"I imagine that it must be. So what do we do now, oh great Greek master? This lowly and very dull Roman slave would like to know," The Sicillian said in a mocking tone, unable to resist chiding his friend for his earlier words about him.

"You know that I only spoke in that manner to protect you," the Greek hold his friend with all sincerity. "Those men would have never accepted you otherwise, they may have even killed you outright as a spy."

"But 'dull'"? Rufus chimed in showing more annoyance than he felt, playing his friend and mentor a bit.

"I know, but who would believe it? Let it be for now. It is of no consequence. We are now in the city, we have made it this far, but Lord Xenophon's execution worries me…"

"Yes, and his execution was on the orders of the Prince—the Prince who hates Rome. I wonder, did he know the truth that his lord was an agent of Rome and Caesar?" the Greek said aloud. "And what did he get out of the lord before he had the man killed?"

"That troubles me as well, but it might also be something else? Perhaps his execution was for some other matter?" Rufus offered hopefully, for the man's execution could have been for some other reason. The Prince was noted as a bloody monster who had men killed often at a whim, or for unusual reasons that were inscrutable to most normal people. It could have been for any reason at all.

"That may very well be, the Prince is said to be short of temper and prone to violence, much like his father the king," Apollodorous told him. Then he shrugged, "Perhaps even mad? At any rate we shall soon find out. Come, let us approach the palace of Lord Xneophon and find out what we can find out."

The two men dismounted, tied their horses and walked towards the arched gate of the wall that surrounded the home of the former Parthian lord. The home was truly a palace and there were armed guards on duty there as well.

"Who are you and what is your business here?" the closest guard demanded in a no nonsense tone.

"We have journeyed a long distance to see Lord Xenophon!" Apollodorous demanded in a rather cheeky tone.

The Sicillian looked carefully at his mentor. They had heard that the Parthian lord was dead, executed by the Prince Tiridates. Was that true? What game was the Greek playing here now, Rufus wondered. Then it came to him. The palace was guarded, as if still occupied, so that meant that the reason Lord Xenophon had been executed by the prince might have had nothing to do with Rome or their mission at all. The family still lived in their home, so he had been executed for some other reason that had nothing to do with his ties to Rome. Or so it appeared.

Rufus wondered what the true reason for the man's execution had been, but as long as it had nothing to do with them and their mission, it meant nothing to him. He did not know that they would find this out soon enough. They found it out when the guard informed them that the Lord Xenophon, The Younger, was in mourning over the death of his father and would see no one.

The Greek though this news over for a moment most carefully, then nodded thoughtfully. What to do now? This was interesting information, a younger Lord Xenephon? How to proceed now? The two travelers looked at each other thoughtfully, but said not a word to each other, fearing secret listeners.

The guard captain came over impatiently, growled at them, "Come on, move away, you two have no business here! Move away or you shall be moved away by force!"

The promise of impending bloody violence was clear.

"Come, Rufus, let us leave these good men to their duty," Apollodorous told his companion in a light-hearted manner so the guards could hear, and then the two men quickly moved off.

"And do not return!" the captain growled impatiently.

When they had moved away far enough to be out of the hearing of the guards, Apollodorous spoke up to Rufus, "This is certainly a strange and unexpected turn of events. What to do now? That is the question. There is a new young Lord. I wonder what that means?"

"I wonder what he knows?" The Sicillian asked carefully.

The Greek shrugged, who could say. Then he added, "I do not believe that *our* Lord Xenophon was executed by the Prince because of his secret business with us and Rome. Were that the case, I am sure the entire family would suffer for any type of perceived treason to the king—or the prince. It appears that the elder lord, nor the family have done anything of the kind to get them all killed."

"Yes, I agree, or they would not still be here, but where does that leave us? Now there is a new Lord Xenophon, the Younger. What does that mean for us? I think we must seek him out at all cost as soon as we can do so," the Greek replied thoughtfully.

"And how do we do that?" The Sicillian asked.

"Why, one of us must get past the household guards and get into that palace and seek him out and then speak to him. We must convince him to help us in our mission," Apollodorous said with all candor.

The Sicillian smiled grimly. "One of us, eh? I have a feeling that means me."

"Of course, for you are young, supple, full of vim and vigor, the perfect man for such an exciting adventure."

"Exciting adventure, eh?"

"Of course."

"More likely an adventure that will get me killed or captured," Rufus said with a sarcastic laugh. He was not against the action, just giving back to the Greek some of what he had given to him hours before when he introduced him to the guards as his 'dull and dim-witted slave.'

"Oh, do not be so grim, my lad," the Greek said in an effort to cheer him up.

"Hah, and what about yourself?"

"Why, my boy, I shall give you my best wishes and prayers to mighty Zeus and all the gods far out here in the East, as I watch diligently for treachery from these guards here. If the guards are alerted and come for you, then I shall act."

"Ah, yes! Well that is a source of great comfort to me, Apollodorous."

The Greek smiled broadly, "I knew that it would be, lad."

The Sicillian laughed cynically, actually enjoying the irony and grim humor exhibited by his friend and mentor, they often shared this dark or sarcastic banter when on a dangerous mission. It helped to relieve the tension. "All right, then I might as well be off. I hope that they do not have any guard dogs on the grounds.

"I do not believe that they do. I did not see or hear any."

The Sicillian shrugged, he knew he would find out about that soon enough.

"The wall on the south side is obscured by tall trees and hedges. I believe it would make an excellent area to attempt your entrance onto the palace grounds."

"Glad you are always thinking of me and my challenges," The Sicillian said with a light laugh.

"Of course, my lad, that is what I am here for," the Greek answered with a wry grin. "Sage advice, after all, I have been your mentor since your youth in Sicily."

"No need to remind me!"

"That is a most cruel barb, my lad."

"All right, all right, well there it is, I see the spot. I believe you are correct," The Sicillian told his companion as he made himself ready, changing into dark clothing, with a long black cape. Leaving his *gladius* short sword behind, he took up a sharp dagger. That is all he should need for tonight's work. If the gods were with him.

"Where do I find this Lord Xenophon, the Younger?"

Apollodorous smiled slightly then shrugged, "Somewhere in that vast pile, no doubt. Search out the most sumptuous rooms or suite, I am sure that he would choose those as his sleeping chambers. I wish you well, my boy. Remember, Caesar and our mission depends upon you now. We are seeking to stop a war from beginning, a war that I am sure even now is heating up on the border. That firebrand Agrippa can not wait to set loose his legions and I fear it will precipitate a disaster for us all. Good luck, Rufus."

The Sicillian nodded, checked his clothing and outfit once more, gave the Greek a lopsided grin and started off.

"If you are captured, my boy," his companion added swiftly, "tell them you are merely a thief come to steal from the house of a wealthy man. That may offer you a quick death, or prison, rather than torture if they believe you to be a spy."

"Thank you, that certainly makes me feel much better about this action."

"Just trying to be helpful, my lad," the Greek replied in a whisper. Then he added, "If by some ill luck the worst does happen, rest assured that I shall mourn you as if you were my very own son. I shall praise your bravery and exploits to Caesar when next I see him."

"Well now, that makes all the difference, doesn't it? I feel so much better. As you and Caesar no doubt will drink fine wine from golden goblets, to my fond memory," The Sicillian replied softly with a wide grimace. But it was of no matter, he was not angered, this type of banter was the usual fun for these two friends. Grim humor, that belied the friendship and affection the two warriors held for each other.

The Greek came back with the low voiced response, "Of course, oh such callow youth, one must never allow the finer things in life to be lost because of any sad event, or over mourning over lost friends."

"You Greeks are some type of people, it is a wonder you ever defeated Xerxes and his Persians."

"I think about that myself sometimes. Now get ready, and be gone, and good luck to you!"

CHAPTER X

In an instant The Sicillian was gone and away, lost into the inky blackness of the city night. He quickly scaled the wall around the huge home and found himself in what appeared to be some richly designed and well groomed garden. The varied delicious scents of wild flowers came strongly to his nostrils. The place was richly appointed. There were statues, many nude and of an erotic nature, and small alcoves all over the grounds, apparently where lovers might seek a private moment. He realized he was in some sort of Parthian pleasure garden. He had heard about such things in the far East back in Rome. He moved forward carefully, wondering where in Hades he might find this Lord Xenophon, the Younger, and what exactly he would say to the man when he did find him.

As it turned out, he did not have long to wait.

The Sicillian was soon attracted by some commotion at the far end of the garden near the house. Drapes were suddenly opened and light was shined outside into the dark night of the garden. The Sicillian quickly hid behind some thick shrubs and then saw a well dressed young man and a lovely young woman come out onto what appeared to be a flowered patio that opened onto the larger environs of the pleasure garden.

The Sicillian watched carefully as the young man and woman moved closer to where he was hiding, they were walking slowly and speaking intently in low tones, but he could hear every word quite clearly. And he listened most intently. They were not speaking in the Parthian tongue, but in Latin, in the Roman tongue, which surprised Rufus even more, as he drew closer so he could listen without missing a word.

The young man and woman were arguing, but in hushed whispers, and at first Rufus thought it to be nothing more than some lovers quarrel. Then he heard General Agrippa and the Armenians mentioned and his ears really perked up at what was being said.

"The Romans are on the way. As we have always feared. The invasion we have prepared for, for many years has finally come. We will be at war and the king is even fearful of the outcome of such a struggle," the young man spoke up softly, but not so soft as that The Sicillian could not hear all his words clearly. He listened most interested.

"Yes, but Prince Tiridates is eager for the fight, eager for more death," the woman responded sadly. "More dead Romans and Parthians and he cares little for the families of the fallen on both sides."

"The beast! He murdered my father. It was not an execution, it was plain murder, pure and simply," the young man said in heated anger.

"He is mad, My Lord." the woman said in a fearful whisper.

"I know," the man replied softly.

"Be calm, My Lord," the woman advised carefully.

"But I had to do it," he cried. "I had no choice. All my family was in danger. My mother, the babies, all of them—even you."

"I know, My Lord, no one knows that more than I do. You did what you had to do. You had no choice. You had to go against your father. Such is the mind madness of the Prince that he brings that out in all who cross his path. But be calm now. Come to me. Best take in the fresh air and clear your head, then come back inside when you are in better spirits. I shall be awaiting you. I know you need some time alone with your thoughts. Be brave."

"You are a good and faithful wife, Alara," he told the young woman as he kissed her gently and then she went back into the house.

The young lord was now alone on the patio in the back of the house, but unknown to him there were *two* secret listeners. The grounds were extensive and The Sicillian, lately joined by Apollodorous looked on with much interest about what they had just heard. The Greek had soon joined his comrade and had heard most of what had been spoken between the Parthian lord and his wife. He handed his companion his short sword and scabbard.

"Thank you. You are late," The Sicillian whispered into his companion's ear.

"I had trouble getting over the damn wall," the Greek replied in a silent tone. "You did not think I was going to let you come in here on your own, did you?"

The Sicillian nodded his head. He knew his friend had his back.

The Greek whispered carefully, "This lord must not have any love for the Prince."

"It surely seems that way. Perhaps we can approach him and he will be of help to us?"

The Greek thought that over for a moment. Finally he looked at his young Roman friend and nodded, whispering, "It seems we have no choice. Let us approach him now while he is alone, but carefully, lest he think we are some assassins or thieves."

The two men were about to make their move when from out of the darkness another voice whispered to them, "That is not advisable, my friends."

The Greek froze, but his hand moved towards the hilt of his sword, The Sicillian quickly drew his dagger.

"No!" the low voice whispered sharply, low but with great force behind it. "I am a friend. Caution!"

The Greek and Roman froze. They could not pinpoint where the soft whispering voice came from. Somewhere behind them for sure, but where? The place was covered in trees and shrubs and offered a multitude of places for a cunning man to hide. The voice was male, but low and whispering in careful subterfuge. The Greek and Roman each grabbed their weapons but the newcomer told them to hold off on any action.

They did.

As of the moment, the Parthian lord had heard nothing of the new-comers in his garden. He was too engaged in his own dark thoughts.

The newcomer whispered softly, like a light breeze upon the wind, "I am a friend. I am a slave in this house, and I am the one you were to meet here, not the old lord, nor his son. Now do you understand?"

"Then come out and show yourself," the Greek told the hidden man.

The man did as he was commanded and now showed himself by walking boldly into the tiny glade in the back of the great house. It was a small secluded area where no one could see them. It was perfect—for stealth talking—or murder—if need be.

"Who are you?" The Sicillian demanded of the man. He noted the man was older, gray hair, barrel-chested, a tough old bird, definitely a slave as his garb indicated, but there was something else about him that made both men—the Roman and the Greek—listen to the man's words. For this slave had eyes of iron and an aura of power and pride about him. He was surely a slave but he had never been conquered as such. He seemed nothing like any of the slaves either of them had known back in Rome. The Sicillian figured it out soon enough.

"You were a gladiator, once?" he asked the man.

The man returned a grim smile of acknowledgement.

"Well?" the Roman demanded in a low whisper.

"Yes, I was once, serving under the Devine Julius, who set me free. I returned to my home here in Ctesiphon, to become a slave once again as I fell on ill fortune, but I always had a special place in my heart for Caesar and Rome—who had been good to me and had set me free. That is why I made it known that I was here to help you."

"And you were the person we were to contact, not your Lord, the deceased one, or his son?"

"Yes, I am that man."

"Then how could you tell that we were the men sent to meet you? The Greek asked his suspicion growing. He did not like this situation, but realized that using his Parthian lord as the supposed spy, offered him some cover. It was the smart move.

The Parthian slave just gave off a grim laugh, "A Roman and a Greek here in the city, in far off Parthia? Who else could you be?" he told them. Then ordering them about, "Come now, we must leave this place. The Prince has spies everywhere. He knows you are coming here and is probably waiting for you to fall into his trap."

"What trap!" The Sicillian demanded.

"Who knows, but he has spies everywhere, so do not assume anything," the man told them.

"Is it true that the old lord was murdered by this mad Prince?" The Sicillian asked.

"Yes, but he was betrayed by his own son. For his son turned his father in to the Prince, repeated words against the prince best left unspoken, if you know what I mean. The young lord had no choice, he did it to protect his wife and family," the slave said. "My name, by the way, is Anon."

Apollodorous smiled at the reference to anonymity. "So we have heard. So be it, Anon. Lead the way. Where to now?"

"To my master's house, to put you in contact with a slave who is in the palace of King Phraates himself. A fellow by the name of Anon the Younger, who will set up a secret audience for you with the King, outside the boundaries and out of the reach of the mad Prince."

"This all seems most strange," The Sicillian told the slave who was leading them to a locked gate, he had some form of key and unlocked the gate and allowed them to pass and enter. Then he took the two men into a street behind the house.

"There is much that is strange these days in Parthia. The King is a good man but old, tired, and the Prince is... Well, he is not so good, a monster really, and he hates all things Roman. So beware. We must speak to the king. He knows, as do we all, that three Roman armies are poised on our western border and they are set to strike soon—if they have not already begun their invasion. It must not happen. We can not have war with Rome now."

"I will say that is true," The Sicillian stated sharply, "for you will lose."

The slave shook his head, "And Rome can not afford a war with Parthia. They will lose too—but no one seems to know that. We must forestall this bloody war. It will be a disaster for us all."

The Sicillian nodded, he agreed with that outcome of a war at this time.

"How do we forestall this war? How do we do that?" the Greek asked as they carefully walked down quiet dark narrow streets and then entered a broad open area that was the city center. There were now magnificent temples and palaces everywhere and the slave dutifully pointed out one vast pile that was the most magnificent of all. "That, my friends, is the palace of King Phraates IV. That is our destination. Now be quick and quiet. No one must see or hear us."

The Greek and The Sicillian did as they were told and Anon brought them quickly through the pitch black empty streets to the wall surrounding the palace. It was almost too easy. Here he made some imitation bird sounds that quickly brought another slave who unlocked the small side gate built into a tall wall to let them into the palace grounds.

"This is Anon, the Younger," Anon told his two companions whose hands had still not left the pommel of their swords. Though they were ever ready for treachery, this all seemed so strange that it actually rang with the reality of truth. Or so it seemed—and so they hoped. Still and all, they were ready for any treachery, and both slaves knew it as well. All were moving most carefully.

"These are the men from Rome?" the man introduced to them as Anon, the Younger, asked the older man.

"Yes, as promised, I have brought them here. You must keep Prince Tiridates away from them, and somehow bring them into a palace room to speak in secret with the King," Anon told the younger man. It was obvious the two slaves were somehow related by blood.

"I will do the best I can. Now you two, follow me inside quickly. Do not speak. Be quiet. I will take you to a special room. There you must wait."

"Goodbye my friends from Rome," the older Anon told the two men from The Empire. "I leave you in good hands. The best hands."

"Another slave like yourself?" the Greek asked curiously.

"Yes, Anon, the Younger, a slave, and my very own son," Anon told the two travelers.

The Sicillian nodded, it seemed right, he had already noticed that the two slaves seemed to be related in some manner.

Anon left them, and Anon, the Younger guided the two travelers into the King's palace. "Come now, hurry! Follow me. Should we be caught by the Prince's men, it will be death for us all, but only after very severe torture. Follow me. I will take you to a secret room, and the King will see you there soon."

"You seem to have everything worked out," The Sicillian asked the young slave with some surprise.

"We have been working on this plan for some time," Anon, the Younger stated matter-of-factly. "Now hurry, we have little time. The Prince has soldiers and spies everywhere."

The Sicillian and the Greek were brought to a large sumptuous suite of rooms deep inside the palace environs. Here Anon, the Younger left them alone with a warning.

"I shall return as soon as I am able to do so, and I will have with me the man you have come so far to speak with. If the Prince and his men take you, do not give up my name, nor my father's name. It will not save you from the Prince's madness, and it will only place us in the same danger and death. "

The Sicillian nodded, he well understood what the consequences were here of failure. He looked to his companion, and the Greek nodded his ascent as well. If captured, they would not do any talking, no matter what was done to them. It was not a prospect either man liked to think about, though they both agreed it was for the best. If caught by the Prince, nothing could save them and they knew it.

"You seem to have quite a bit of influence here," the Greek asked the slave before he left the room.

"We do what we can, but as slaves our ears and eyes are everywhere, always open," Anon replied, and then he was gone.

The Roman and the Greek nodded at that explanation and they settled down to wait.

CHAPTER XI

"Well," Apollodorous stated with a wry grin, "our fate is in the hands of the gods alone who know…"

"I do not like this, but we do not seem to have a choice in the matter," The Sicillian replied, taking a seat and easing his weary body.

The Greek joined him, there was food and wine on a table and he helped himself to a hearty repast. "Might as well at least enjoy a decent meal for a change. The wine is said to be good out here in the East."

The Sicillian nodded and joined his friend in a light repast.

The two men waited for a couple of hours, talking in low tones among themselves about what they were to do, and how they were to avert the war—and how in Hades they were to accomplish their mission of seeking the release of the captured Roman eagles and standards that Caesar Augustus seemed to desire above all things these days. They did not think they would get much help from the Parthian king, even if he wanted peace—as it was said by Anon. They wondered just what it would take to avert the war, bring success to their mission for Caesar—and get out of this alive with their skins intact.

After more time had passed the two men were alerted when the door to their room slowly and quietly opened and Anon returned to them. He most carefully closed the door behind him as he got the attention of the two men in the room. Their swords were out and ready for treachery, but it was just the young slave. He was alone.

The two travelers lowered their swords, but did not put them away.

"It is I, Anon, returned for you, my friends. All is in readiness," the young slave told the two travelers. "Now, you must come with me, the King awaits."

"It's about time!" the Greek whispered in exasperated impatience.

At that moment the door to the room burst open and through it came a half dozen palace soldiers. The swords of the guardsmen were out and ready and behind them urging them onward was a richly dressed and armored man who looked to be much more than any palace officer or mere guard commander. The man had a cruel look to his eyes, that glowed with mad hatred at the two stunned travelers he found surrounded now by his men. He apparently knew who they were.

"I am Prince Tiridates!" the newcomer announced boldly with blazing eyes glowing with hatred. "Now you Roman dogs shall die! Move on them! Take them! Then you shall be tortured for what you know!" he ordered his men to advance.

The palace guardsmen carefully moved forward with outstretched swords itching to tasted the blood of the two travelers who also had their own swords out and were ready to fight and defend themselves. The Sicillian and the Greek were determined to sell their lives dearly, should it be the will of the gods.

However, the Roman and the Greek needed no such announcement to tell them what was about to happen. The moment the Prince and his men burst into the room they had their swords out and charged upon the palace guardsmen. The Prince ordered his men onward, safely from behind their ranks, and under their protection. He was no fool. Nor was he brave. He drew his sword, but never used it. He made sure never to get close enough to the two Romans to be able to use his sword—or be in peril by their swords.

There were six of the palace guardsmen commanded by the Prince and they were all good fighters, but The Sicillian and Apollodorous soon made quick work of them with superior swordplay and bold attacks. Each of the Romans took out two guardsmen in the close spaces of the room in the initial attack, before the other two guards could get in close and at them. When they did get to meet the swords of the Roman and Greek, these two were also cut down. By that time four of the Prince's guards lay dead upon the floor and a small battle waged between the two remaining guardsmen, with the Prince behind them fearful and shocked at the outcome of what he thought would be a quick and easy victory for his men.

That final fight against the last two guards was fierce—and each man involved in the battle knew it was to the death. The Prince finally moved forward into the fight, and he surprised the two Romans when he proved to be an able swordsman. The Prince entering the fray changed the odds three to two, and he proved to know quite a few dirty tricks and displayed them well, but the wily Sicillian stayed him off. Rufus blocked the Prince's sword, stopping his every attempt to cut him down. Then in lightning strikes The Sicillian dispatched one of the remaining guards, even as the Greek took down the last remaining guardsman. All the guards were down now and the Prince stood alone in front of the Roman and Greek now.

The Parthian Prince remained alone, full of hatred and anger, but suddenly overcome by a terrible fear, now that he realized that he was truly alone. He had proved to be a bully and a coward. He had never suspected the attack on the Roman and Greek would ever turn out this way. He had thought to catch the Greek and Roman unawares, but if anything, they seemed ready and expecting something of the sort. They were ready for him and proved their fighting abilities were superior even to his own guardsmen.

Anon, the Younger, now coming out from a corner of the room, came forward as The Sicillian disarmed the Prince and held him while the Greek set his dagger firmly to the royal throat.

"No! Do not kill him!" Anon pleaded cautiously.

"Why not? He tried to kill us, and he is an enemy of Rome!" the Greek replied allowing his temper to glow now. He was angry at the attack. So was The Sicillian.

"Your man is correct, do not kill him," the voice of an old man in richly appointed garments and wearing a jeweled crown suddenly spoke up from behind them. He had quietly entered the room unseen with a routine of armed guardsmen during the fight, but he had held his men back from interfering. He was Phraates IV, King of Parthia. "He is my eldest son, impetuous and sometimes foolish, but I beg you not to kill him. Stay your bloody hand, Greek!"

Then to back up his request, a group of archers and swordsmen came from behind the king and leveled their arrows at the Roman and Greek. The threat was clear.

"Archers!" The Sicillian whispered to his Greek companion. Both knew what that meant. They might kill the Prince, but there was no escaping this trap now. They could never hope to win a battle against archers. "I hate archers!"

"Great King, we do not wish to kill your son—or anyone at all," Apollodorous spoke up in his most appreciating voice. "We came here to speak to you as representatives of Rome and Caesar Augustus, not to fight your guardsmen or to kill your son. We will gladly turn him loose if you will guarantee our safety and allow us some time to speak with you of peace in private. You must know that three Roman armies at this time are poised to strike through your western border."

"Kill them all! Kill them all now, Father!" the Prince shouted full of anger and hatred. "Archers, shoot these dogs down dead! I command you! Your Prince commands it!"

Apollodorous, pressed the blade of his dagger more deeply to the Prince's throat, ready for come what may. The Sicillian stood ready with his *gladius*, set to burst into the group of archers and cut them down as best he might.

"Halt! Only I command here, Tiridates, not you—*not yet!* Archers stay your arrows. You two from Rome, release my son and I promise no harm shall come to you and we shall have the time you request alone to speak of peace. If you and the man you serve truly deserve it, for Peace is very dear to my heart."

Apollodorous nodded and moved his dagger blade away from the Prince's throat. The Sicillian released his hold and the Prince, appearing more like a spoiled brat—ran out of the room over to his father.

"How could you! Kill them now!"

"Be silent, my son," the King ordered in a firm voice that belied his advanced age. The King was an old man, but he still had a lot of fire in him, when necessary. It was necessary now. Phraates was still very much in command here. "Tiridates, you will leave me now, and take these guards with you—before I give you the punishment you deserve for such a traitorous act! Perpetrated here in my very palace! Consider yourself blessed that you are my son, and not one of my subjects or soldiers. I still rule here, Tiridates, and what I say goes!"

The young Prince, soundly chastened in front of the Greek, Roman, and the palace guards by the King, silently went off alone not waiting for the guard escort. His face was twisted into a rectus of pain and anger but he knew better than to offend his regal father at this time, so he was soon gone out of the room. His guardsmen, those alive and dead, were carted off with him by the king's men.

"That one will be more trouble for the king as time goes on," The Sicillian whispered to his elder friend thoughtfully.

"Yes, and for Rome and Caesar as well," the Greek responded in a low tone.

Apollodorous and The Sicillian collected their weapons, armor and cloaks and followed the king and his men out of the suite of rooms and into a large hall. They were escorted by the king's guards, but respectfully. Anon, the Younger, was sent away, but not before the king told him in a friendly tone, "You have done well this day. I thank you."

"It is my pleasure to serve you, oh Great King," Anon replied with all humility.

"And Rome as well?" the king asked him curiously.

Anon look extremely uncomfortable, but the king gave him a wan smile, "Speak up, man"

"Sometimes a man may have two masters and serve both equally well, My King," Anon replied with a bow of his head. "I serve Parthia—and the cause of peace—not Rome."

"Ah, yes, as do I. Very well, then be on your way now, Anon, the Younger, and give my regards to your father," King Phraates told the slave with a nod of his regal head. Then the king and his men led The Sicillian and the Greek down a long corridor into the bowels of the royal palace.

"Where are we going?" Apollodorous asked the king carefully, a bit fearful that they might be taken to some dark prison cell to cool their heels. Perhaps the king had had a change of heart upon these matters? Such a change in plans and temperament were not uncommon among kings and the powerful, regardless of what they said—or even promised.

"Fear not, Good Greek, we are going to my private apartments where we may discuss the problems between Rome and Parthia—Caesar and I—in better surroundings. More privately."

The Greek only nodded. He and Rufus still wore their weapons—both swords and daggers—which had not been taken away from them, so they felt somewhat secure and safe. At least for the moment. That at least, was a good sign.

The Sicillian and Apollodorous were led by the king and his guards to a enormous and sumptuous suite of rooms deep within the palace, and here the king and his two 'guests' were seated in comfort and relaxation.

"Slaves will bring us food and drink," the king spoke up, even as a bevy of lovely young ladies brought in what was sure to be a veritable feast of amazing food and victuals. The young ladies deftly placed everything on a large table before the three men, then quietly left the room without a sound.

"They are lovely, are they not?" the Parthian king asked with a wide grin. It was obvious he appreciated the female form.

"Most agreeable, oh King, in fact, rather delectable," the Greek replied with a wary leer at the last young lady as she sauntered off. It was obvious the wily Greek had taken a shine to her.

Rufus, only nodded, thinking of his Lady Octavia, and wishing that it would not be too long before he saw her again. Still and all, he did notice the lovely ladies and appreciated their beauty as much as his friend and the old king did.

"You may have your pick of any one of them, my friends,' the king told his guests. "Or, perhaps, have all of them at once!"

The wily Greek smiled, but said nothing.

The King gave out a deep laugh, "I am old, my foxing days are well past me, but I can still look upon the ladies and appreciate what the gods have given us in the female form."

"Of course, my King!" Apollodorous replied, he was getting to like this old king, even if an enemy of Rome.

The Sicillian just nodded in agreement, still thinking of his lady Octavia and how he missed her more than ever.

"It is just as well. Regardless, now we are here in safety, comfort, with good food and drink," the king spoke up in a calm tone. "Now we can properly discuss our little problems."

The Greek nodded with a wry smile.

The Sicillian said nothing as of yet. They were waiting for the king to continue to express his thoughts. What did he want? What did Parthia want?

"So, I ask you, truthfully, why are you two men here? And why do the Romans position three armies on my western border? See, I know of the impending invasion, my spies are, if I may say so with some pride, far better than your own spies. I have known of your plans for many days. I have even been aware of your secret mission to seek me out. So tell me now, out with it, what can be done to forestall this war? As far as I know you Romans have not yet attacked, nor entered Parthian territory, which is to the good, though I hear your brave General Agrippa strains at the leash Caesar has placed upon him to begin an attack and the invasion."

The Sicillian shook his head slightly, it seemed the Parthian king knew far more than they gave him credit for. He wondered what the king knew that he had not yet said?

"That is true," the Greek spoke up calmly, helping himself to a goblet of fine Persian wine. The wine makers in this part of the world rivaled the Greeks themselves in their fine victuals. Apollodorous smiled, "When The Sicillian and I left Caesar, many days ago, the attack had not yet begun. I am happy to hear that in the intervening time, it has not yet happened. I am sure, however, that time is running very short."

"Yes," King Phraates nodded in agreement. "Time is running out to keep the peace."

"We have come to help you to keep the peace," the Greek spoke up serious now. "Will you hear us out?"

"Yes, I will hear you out, for I also seek peace with Rome. But does Rome seek peace with Parthia? That is yet to be determined. Peace is always better created that way. Both sides must be in agreement with the desire to have peace."

"You are a wise king, Phraates," The Sicillian spoke up sincerely.

"I am an old king, young pup, but it may be true that some wisdom does come with age. Now what do you want? What does your Caesar want?"

The Sicillian and Apollodorous both looked carefully at the king. The Greek spoke up first. He began, "Caesar is a great leader…"

The king quickly interjected, "Who would like nothing better than to add Persia and other parts of my domain under Roman rule, but it shall not happen. Caesar can not win here in the far East—your supply lines will not allow it. Two times before, under the able Crassus, and then under the noble Antony, Rome tried to conquer Parthia, and failed. It was a fiasco. Crassus lost a total of seven of your precious legions, did he not?"

The two men did not need the king of remind them of the two Roman defeats here in Parthia that was still a fresh wound on both sides even many years later. They need not be reminded of the fact that Crassus lost seven legions—and that Crassus himself was forced to drink molten gold and die at the hands of his Parthian enemies.

Rufus and Apollodorous were silent for a long moment, thinking things through.

Finally the Greek said, "That it true and you still hold in your possession as trophies of those victories certain Roman legion eagles and standards. Do you not?"

"You know that I do. Yes, that is true," the king spoke up swiftly, with some pride in his voice. "I have those dusty old mementos, somewhere here in the palace, and I am holding on to them to remind us of our gallant victories over Rome. We also hold some Roman prisoners from those long ago battles. Rome was foolish to invade Parthia, their generals overbold and arrogant. They lost both wars back then, and should Caesar Augustus do so again, he will meet with the same result for a third time."

"Perhaps?" Apollodorous stated calmly, not showing much doubt in his tone. He smiled, looked over at The Sicillian.

Rufus nodded, as to their prearranged plan, he now spoke up, "That may all be true Great King, but Great Caesar is not like anyone you have ever dealt with before, he is like a hungry wolf and has three Roman armies poised to invade at your western border. These include his own legions, also Tiberius in the north, and the wily Agrippa in Armenia, who will also invade with an Armenian army as well. It will be a sight to behold, Agrippa is keen to be let loose. He is a real fighter, that one is."

The king nodded, he knew of the reputation of the Roman general as a first-rate military strategist and tactician. Marcus Vipsanius Agrippa was deemed a military genius.

Then Apollodorous asked in all innocence, "But why have war? Is it really necessary? War is nasty, bloody, a brutal business, and it results in all manner of calamity. Sometimes the results can not be planned, so in the heat of war all kinds of nasty surprises often spring up. Unexpected. Very bad surprises. Instability and chaos among our nations being the worse. Is it really necessary? Why not just give Great Caesar that which he wants the most."

"Never! I shall not give up one speck of Parthian territory!" the king bristled with a growing anger. Then he continued, "I still consider the Roman buffer and client kingdom of Armenia as belonging to Parthia. It had been carved out of territory once under our rule long ago."

"That was long ago," The Sicillian answered coyly, "but we shall not solve that problem here now. We have another more pressing problem we need to address."

The king looked at the two men in repressed anger but did not reply.

"But Great King, we are here to tell you that Great Caesar seeks not one speck of Parthian territory as any tribute to avert war. He seeks no land from you at all. In fact, he would rather avoid war at all costs—if possible. A wise course, I am sure you agree, especially seeing that your own empire is receiving severe pressure from your own barbarians far off in the East. The Huns and other eastern peoples of the steppes. And then there are those Mongols. I am told they are most formidable horsemen and quite disagreeable and deadly."

King Phraates sighed and nodded with some reluctance, it was true about the problems Parthia faced in the far East. The Mongols were a particular concern. "That is no secret. There is always the pressure of outside invasion. So what is it that Caesar wants so much that he will forestall his invasion?"

"Rather simple really, Great King," the Greek spoke up in a soft conciliatory voice. "He would like the Roman legion eagles and standards that you hold be returned to him as a gesture of good will and friendship. And then he and his armies with withdraw—for he has other matters to deal with in his own empire—as I am sure that you do as well. Both armies could be better utilized at home, than in battle against each other. War between Rome and Parthia would solve nothing I fear but weaken both great nations only to the betterment of our enemies."

The Sicillian added casually, "Oh, and Caesar would appreciate it if any Roman army prisoners taken from those past incursions could be returned as well, should they wish to return to their homes."

The Parthian king sat stone faced, and both men wondered just what he was thinking. Finally he nodded and said, "These trophies of victory are meaningful to us—to me—but if their return to Caesar can create his good will…"

"They will, Great King," the Greek chimed in quickly and firmly.

The Parthian king sat rigid, silent, thoughtful. Finally he just nodded and said, "Then he can have them. We care little for them in reality. They collect dust in my Great Hall. And he may have the remaining prisoners as well. There are a scant dozen left from Antony's days. Take them all and tell Caesar to remove his armies from our western border, and we shall remove our army from his own eastern border."

"That is wise, Great King," The Sicillian spoke up. "Caesar and Rome thank you."

The Sicillian looked at his Greek companion, nodded.

The Greek spoke up, "And when may we be given the eagles and standards? For Caesar will want them returned to him straight away, and me and my young companion here must leave as soon as possible to present them to him," the Greek added, trying to tamp down his impatience. He knew they had to move fast on this, but they could not appear too eager.

King Phraates waved his hands casually, as if it was nothing of any consequence, "You can have them all now, if you like, and then you may leave to take them to Caesar this very day. Take them and go."

Then the king called in his guardsmen and ordered them to bring in the eagles and standards of the Roman legions they held captive—captured in battles with Crassus and Antony. "Your captured men will be returned by a wagon under guard of my soldiers in the coming days. Will that be satisfactory to Caesar?"

"Great King, I am sure that will prove most satisfactory," Apollodorous spoke up with a broad smile, a smile which grew as soldiers of King Phraates now brought into the room two large bundles of dusty wooden and metal poles upon which proudly stood gold Roman legionary eagles, and somewhat faded flags and pennants, the standards of the various centuries and cohorts of the legions who had invaded Parthia decades before—legions that had all been defeated.

"These shall all be returned to Caesar. Take them with you now, and assure him of our everlasting friendship," the King spoke up with a careful smile.

"At least for now," the Greek said softly with a wily grin.

The king heard the Greek and nodded back.

The Greek smiled, knowingly, for he well understood the way of things in the world.

"Yes, Greek, friendship...at least for now," the King answered back with what looked to be a wily grin.

Nevertheless, the deal was settled and the exchange made.

The Sicillian accepted the bundles from the Parthian guards, happy but not showing his happiness too broadly, but this was indeed a treasure trove for Caesar and Rome. It was in truth the missing eagles and standards of the lost Roman legions. It was a magnificent act—and a great victory. And to have them returned without war was nothing short of Devine. Truly the majesty of Caesar Augustus had the power to move even the Parthian King to...a form of cooperation.

The Sicillian said, "We thank you, for Caesar and Rome."

"Yes, I thank you, and Caesar thanks you as well, Great King," Apollodorous added with his sage humility as The Sicillian gathered up their bundled goods. "Caesar will be most pleased."

"Most pleased, so that he does not see my gracious magnanimity as a blundering weakness, and that he instead sees the return of these military icons as the actions of a friend. If so, I will be happy. With that in mind he should now remove his three armies from the border of my empire—that is the results I crave for this show of my *friendship*," Phraates spoke up forcefully. There was also an unmistakable menace in his voice, should the deal made here today not prove to be true. Would Caesar honor it? The Greek was not all that sure, neither was The Sicillian. This generosity could, in fact, actually cause a war by showing perceived weakness or fear. Caesar made up his own rules as he went along, so no one could truly say what he would do in this situation.

"Great King, I am sure that your generosity and wisdom shall not fail you this day. Now, I and my young companion, must leave at once to bring this most welcome news and take these wonderful gifts from you to our Great Caesar."

"Then go now, my friends, my soldiers will escort you to the borders of Parthia," the king told them, and he was as good as his word.

Within the hour The Sicillian and Apollodorous were riding their steeds westward through the Parthian plains towards the border with Rome. The Sicillian still rode his trusty Batavian warhorse. The Greek had a smaller but more agile Eastern mount. Both men spurred their horses onward to the West, accompanied by a troop of palace guardsmen ordered to escort them safely under protection by the Parthian King. The two men could not have asked for a more perfect solution to their mission. They only wondered how Caesar would react...

The two men rode quickly, both leading one large pack horse, that was carrying the eagles and standards of the defeated Roman legions. Their return would herald a momentous victory for Caesar and Rome. The two men rode like the wind, nonstop. The entire troop, accompanied by Parthian palace guardsmen, had been riding hard and fast, non-stop.

Two days later their Parthian escort left them, the commander telling the two travelers, "The Roman camp is below in yonder valley, barely two hours away. They have not moved eastward yet into Parthian territory—see that they never do. Good luck, I and my men now take our leave of you. It has been most interesting."

"Thank you for your protection through your country," the Greek told them.

The Parthian commander nodded, grimly, "Just see to it that your Caesar does what he is supposed to do."

The Greek smiled, nodded to the commander in his most friendly manner, but in truth, he did not know at all how to answer that question. So he said nothing to the commander.

Once the Parthian soldiers were gone, Apollodorous spoke up to his companion, "Now we head to Caesar's headquarters camp and present him with the returned eagles and standards. He will be most pleased."

"I am sure he will be," The Sicillian said, "but I wonder…"

"You wonder? Wonder about what, my lad?" the Greek asked as they led their horses down a small defile into the valley on route to the encampment of the Roman army.

"I wonder if Caesar will see the return of the eagles and standards as a sign of weakness, and as a result, push forward with the attack into Parthian territory. I would put nothing beyond him. If he can take Persia, it would be a mighty victory. I know he is desirous of that land."

"That is what I am thinking myself, young man," Apollodorous said thoughtfully. His face looked grim. "Caesar may already be planning to go to war even as we speak. He is certainly ready for war. He has always had desires upon Persia. The legions are ready. Tiberius and Agrippa are ready. To stop it all at this point would be most difficult now that all the pieces are here, in place and ready to go."

"Only a truly great leader could do such a thing now—by attacking—or holding off an attack. I guess we shall see soon enough," The Sicillian stated knowingly. Curious and concerned. Wondering what Caesar would do. Augustus, was truly the son of the Devine Julius if not in blood, then in spirit. He was smart and bold and capable of almost anything. Rufus knew the *Princips* better than most did, so anything here was indeed possible.

"Yes, and so I have a feeling we shall soon see how great a leader our young Caesar truly is. Hurry, I see Roman auxiliary cavalry coming towards us. Let's meet them and then have them take us to Caesar immediately."

CHAPTER XII

Caesar Augustus, was awash in joy and absolute happiness at the good news, "Rufus! Apollodorous! You have returned! I feared you lost. Truly! And I know you have something for me from King Phraates. What does that old Parthian dog have for me that I could ever want? What gift? What sheer bauble? Surely not the eagles and standards I crave and have so often demanded of him?"

"The very same, mighty Caesar!" the Greek replied with a wide grin, a victorious grin that he proudly showed now. It was the grin of victory. Two of Caesar's soldiers carefully brought into the huge tent some large cloth-covered bundles that contained the returned Roman Army legionary eagles and standards.

"You have them! Here, now! He returned them to you! By the gods!" Caesar shouted elated as he went over to the bundles and ran his hands lovingly over the legionary icons, almost caressing them with love and joy. "This is incredible! Surely no one would believe such a thing possible? And we did not even have to go to war to regain them! For if all truth be told now, I was never going to give the order to advance into Parthia. Why do you both look at me like that? Think I am a fool? Goodly Agrippa was wild with frustration that we did not move forward, now I shall have to order him to fall back. He will not like that, but he will do as I tell him, now that I have what I want."

"Yes, Caesar," the Greek answered him with a winning smile at their success, and that war had indeed been averted.

The Sicillian nodded in agreement, for he was happy that all had turned out well enough and now his thoughts ran once again to seeing Octavia and spending some time with her. When he had first left her to take on this mission he had never thought that he would ever return. Now he was back in the Empire and he looked forward to the future and time spent with Octavia again—but their liaison must be taken quietly and away from the prying eyes of her brother and his ever-present spies.

Caesar Augustus smiled broadly once more, for he was indeed most happy at the outcome of this venture. The bundles had been unwrapped and he continued to run his hands across the eagles and standards, his face brimming with triumph. "This is indeed a great victory. When I bring these icons back to Rome and present them to the People and Senate I will see to it that there will be a grand triumphal parade throughout the city. Furthermore, I shall see to it that coins are minted to commemorate this momentous event. And all shall sing the praises of what has been accomplished here this day—and without war, without one battle fought, and without one Roman soldier killed. This is truly a good day, my friends."

"And, there is even more, Caesar, for Phraates promised to return by wagon in a few days the prisoners taken in the ill-fated invasion by Antony," the Greek added.

Caesar nodded, "Then doubly good, that is, a true reason to celebrate!"

"Then Caesar is happy at the outcome?" the Greek asked curiously.

Caesar Augustus nodded his regal head, smiled broadly, then looked at the wily Greek with a look just as wily. "Of course. However, it does make me wonder, though. Why is that old dog Phraates being so accommodating? Were I of a more suspicious mind, or a cunning one, I might take this move as a sign of great weakness. Perhaps even fear. Surely Agrippa will, and he will press me to order the attack. So perhaps I should order our armies to move immediately? Perhaps this is the time in history when we should act?"

"No, Caesar, it is not!" The Greek said softly.

"No?" Caesar enquired slowly, looking curiously at the Greek and The Sicillian.

Apollodorous grew grim, The Sicillian looked at him with grave concern, this is what both men had been afraid of, and both men looked at Caesar with growing concern. Was Caesar actually now considering ordering an attack upon Parthia? Surely not now? Had the return of the eagles and standards done the reverse of what it had been intended to accomplish? Instead of forestalling a war no one truly wanted, had it shown weakness that might bring about the very war so many had tried to avert?

"Well, my friends? What do you have to say?" Caesar asked in a soft tone.

The Greek looked at The Sicillian with a sharp leer that told him to tread carefully here. Neither man spoke up for a long moment, thinking things through as best they could. What were their options? They had none.

The Greek and The Sicillian grew nervous as they looked upon Caesar Augustus. The leader of the world remained silent, apparently deeply thinking the situation through, taking in all the various possibilities. To conquer Parthia—to destroy Parthia—was a powerful drug to any Roman general or leader to take. Was victory possible? Both men knew Caesar was, in fact, actually now considering the action. They looked carefully upon Caesar Augustus. What was in his thoughts, they wondered? This one man was the sole ruler of their world, he made war or kept the peace by his very whim. It was all up to him now. What would he decide?

Caesar suddenly shook his head and smiled broadly, "You know, I never truly planned for war, my friends. This movements of the legions, even unto my coming out here to the East, was all for show, an attempt to put pressure upon the Parthians to give up our military icons at the threat of invasion. So they thought I would invade? Now there is no reason to do so, and I shall never fall into that trap, the trap that Crassus and Antony fell into so many years ago. I am smarter than that. And I am not so greedy for fame and power. I have enough of both, thank you."

"You are wise, Caesar," Apollodorous uttered in a loud cry of relief, adding, "Praise be you, Caesar Augustus!"

"So you old reprobate, you thought I was going to invade?"

"The thought did cross my mind, My Lord."

Caesar Augustus laughed lightly, shrugged, " Indeed, it did cross my mind as well. It would be an interesting outcome, a gamble with all chips upon the table in one big pot. One can never win a great victory without taking great risk. Perhaps I should give the order? What do you think? And you as well, Rufus? You have been most quite lately."

The Greek and The Sicillian suddenly grew nervous once again. They shook their heads solemnly, indicating the negative in the strongest terms.

Caesar saw their reaction and just laughed in a good-natured manner, "No, fear not my friends, we are done with war here in the East. I have no taste for it. Another reason is that of late I have heard disturbing news from our lands in far off Germania. It seems a similar problem as this one has lately come up, most vexing I will tell you, and I want you both to go there immediately and find out the truth of it. Solve it for me. One way, or the other."

"Germania?" the Greek asked carefully, utterly surprised.

"Yes, Germania," Caesar replied firmly. The request was not a request, but an order and all three men knew it.

"May I ask, what is the particular problem, Caesar?" The Sicillian spoke up cautiously. Most curious now. Wondering what else could go wrong—and when would he see Octavia?

"Well, I am sure it is nothing that the two of you can not handle. One of our legions in Germania has something important that has gone lost and since you both have vast experience in the finding of lost items, this is a matter for you both to correct. I have the utmost faith in you, so I am sending you both to Germania to solve the problem. Immediately. You leave at dawn."

"What problem exactly?" The Sicillian insisted, fearing the answer.

"I believe you are being vague purposefully, Caesar," Apollodorous dared to speak up, allowing a grimace to cross the weathered features of his face.

"Indeed, well it may be complicated, and if I told you the truth of it now, you might not even believe my words. You shall find out about it soon enough. I suggest you rest tonight and then leave at first light tomorrow. Germania is a long way off and a hard ride for even fast riders. And you must ride fast. When you finish this mission, meet me again in Rome and we shall spend some time together. Now leave me alone with my eagles and standards, they speak to me of battles won and lost and many of our brave valiant legionnaires gone to the grave. I would honor them alone, in my own way."

Apollodorous and The Sicillian left Caesar's tent and were taken by his guards to a tent of their own where they would sleep a fitful night.

"Germania? Of all the grim dark places! What in Hades are we being sent there for?" The Sicillian asked his friend gravely.

"Something to do with the legions there, I suspect. A revolt? War? Maybe an invasion? Caesar was purposefully vague, I wonder why."

"I can not be good," The Sicillian said before sleep overtook him.

"No, of a certainty I think I can promise you that it can not be good," the Greek muttered before he fell into an exhausted sleep.

CHAPTER: XIII

The next morning the Greek and The Sicillian were on their war steeds riding with mad fury in the direction of the wilds of Germania far off towards the north and west of the Empire. They were headed towards Roman Gaul. They each led one pack horse and two remounts and pushed their steeds as fast as they could, but not so much as they would wear out their own warhorses. They changed horses regularly so that no one mount would be too wasted, but as the hours and days went by, the two men grew weary. They did not stop, they did not sleep.

"What in Hades is going on in Germania? I wonder?" The Sicillian asked his Greek mentor while on the ride.

"We shall see soon enough," Apollodorous cryptically replied in an almost scholarly tone. Caesar had been most veiled about it all—as if—embarrassed. Perhaps? Could that be possible? Now what could that mean?

"What do you think? You know something, do you not?" Rufus asked in a firm tone, demanding an answer from his more wise and worldly friend.

Apollodorous just shrugged grimly, "Nothing for sure. I have heard some words. That is all, just rumors. Caesar did not elaborate on it to me—so angered was he by the very hearing of it. He could not speak of it. It may not be true, but he is sending us to discover the truth of the rumor, and if that rumor be true, then remedy it. Either way, it could prove a most difficult mission. Dealing with German barbarians is not like dealing with civilized Parthians, who may be reasoned with in some aspects. Barbarians understand only force, and there my lad, we are slightly deficient being just the two of us."

The Sicillian grimaced, "That sounds as dire and grim as Germania itself. So then what?"

"Well, my young friend, it seems we have been placed in the thick of the soup once again. Our success with having King Phraates return the Roman eagles and standards lost by Crassus and Antony so many years ago, has now made us something of experts in dealing with this type of situation. Much to my regret."

"And what type of situation is that?"

"Well, diplomacy, and such other types of nebulous things. Negotiations, perhaps? The situation of lost legionary eagles is one that is of the utmost importance to Rome and Caesar—regaining them is even better! Who shall see what we will meet when we arrive at the legion encampment in Gaul," the Greek replied grimly as he spurred his horse onto greater speed. It was obvious he did not want to discuss the details of this new matter at this time.

The Sicillian did not accept his friend's response, but he had no choice but to do so for now. He knew he would get no more from his companion until he was ready to speak his mind on the subject. He spurred his mount and caught up with his friend and mentor but demanded an explanation nonetheless.

"Well? Come now, out with it!" the young man demanded of the older man. He would not let it go, so the older man gave a nasty grimace for he knew he had no choice but to come clean on the matter now.

"Well, it seems that *Legio V Alaudae* and their legate, Marcus Lollius have gotten themselves into a bit of a jam in Roman Gaul," Apollodorous said carefully, in what was surely the understatement of the year.

The Sicillian looked warily at his friend, shook his head dubiously, waiting with utter disbelief, and then he asked incredulously, "They lost their eagle?"

"Not lost, I'm afraid, we know where it is. It is in the hands of a German barbarian tribe—but it was taken from the legion in battle."

"Lost in battle!" The Sicillian growled, refusing to accept what he was hearing.

"Yes, I am afraid that might be true."

"How in Hades did that happen?"

"I said it might be true, Rufus. We can not be sure yet."

The Sicillian just shook his head in despair.

"Well, I have not all the facts on the matter, but it seems *Legio V Alaudae* fought some German tribes who raided into Roman Gaul. The raiding party was larger than anyone realized, and the attack hit them harder than anyone expected. The legion broke their ranks and in the confusion they reported that they lost their precious eagle. Caesar is furious."

"No doubt," Rufus acknowledged with a low whistle, he could well imagine Caesar's response, and the punishments that would be forthcoming if such a thing had in fact occurred. "So what does Caesar expect us to do about it?"

"Why, it is rather simple really, he expects us to get his damned eagle back!" the Greek said bluntly.

The Sicillian brought his warhorse to a sudden stop and looked carefully at his friend.

The Greek stopped his own mount and looked back a bit sadly.

"Not again? Is it true?" The Sicillian sighed heavily as the two men continued to ride on in thoughtful silence now that the truth was out. Now Rufus understood why his friend had been less than open with him on this new mission, in an effort to spare him from the dire facts, for at least a little while. They rode on in silence. What did Caesar expect of them? Miracles? They were not soothsayers, nor magicians. They were fighting men!

The two men rode on in silence, neither man wishing to speak for some time. There was not much to say until they reached the legion camp where they would find out exactly what had happened from the legate commander.

The Sicillian and Apollodorous crossed the boundary into Roman Gaul and soon found the headquarters of *Legio V Alaudae*, the 5th Legion Aldadue, and once they showed the guards the proper identifications, were immediately ushered into the presence of the legate, Marcus Lollius.

"So you are here from Caesar Augustus," Lollius asked them carefully. They were now in the legate's spacious tent, and behind his desk where the commander sat confidently, stood what appeared to be the legion's eagle. It was a most welcome sight to behold.

Both newcomers noticed the icon with evident pleasure. So the rumor had *not* been true. So the eagle had *not* been lost! Thank the gods! So what in Hades was going on here?

Apollodorous now smiled broadly, much relieved, and said, "Caesar has heard some silly rumor about you having lost the eagle in some battle with barbarian German tribes out here in Gaul. We are relieved— and I am sure he will be as well—that the story is not true."

"Caesar asked us to investigate the matter," The Sicillian explained further, in a simple statement, relieved to see the golden eagle in Roman hands where it belonged. "I am also happy to find out now that this news has been only a bad rumor and nothing more."

Lollius sighed deeply, shook his head ominously, something was indeed wrong here.

The Sicillian looked at the legate closely, and the Greek made a murmur sound that did not bode well.

The legate spoke up carefully, "Not quite a rumor. In truth, we did lose our eagle—only for a short amount of time—but you can report proudly back to Caesar that I gathered a larger military force and defeated these Germans. My men sent them on their way in a quick battle. They sued for peace and even returned our eagle."

The Sicillian looked at his Greek companion with obvious surprise, both looked at Lollius carefully. They did not know whether to be relieved or horrified. Relived that the imperial eagle had been returned to the legion—or horrified that it had indeed been taken by barbarians in the first place.

"The barbarians returned your legionary eagle?" The Sicillian asked curiously, unbelieving what he had just heard, but seeing the evidence of it there right before his eyes made it true. The legion's eagle stood tall not a dozen feet away from him, on display behind the legate's camp desk. There was no denying the fact.

The Sicillian just shook his head in relief, but he had many questions. These German barbarians did not seem like the accommodating type, even should they be soundly defeated in battle. They were known for never giving up, and they would certainly never give up a Roman legionary eagle should they ever capture one.

Something was wrong here and The Sicillian looked at the legate most carefully trying to think out the meaning of this…puzzle. Or was it a puzzle at all? Perhaps he was making too much of it all? Perhaps it was as the legate had told them, that the barbarians had been soundly beaten and part of their suit for peace had been the return of the legion's eagle. Perhaps it was that simple? Rufus looked over to his Greek friend to see what he thought of this news.

"You are a lucky man, Marcus Lollius," the Greek told the commander in all sincerity. His face was stony, not showing any feelings on the matter. Not yet.

"I need not you to tell me that," the legate replied dryly, as if the matter were settled now and closed. However, there was still Caesar to consider.

"So all is well here then?" The Sicillian asked, allowing some relief to show through. "Then we may leave and report back to Caesar in Rome that *Legio V Alaudae* has been victorious and is in full possession of its eagle and legionary standards?"

"Of course. You may report that to Caesar, yes," the legate stated in a low tone, embarrassed by the admission, but proud that all had worked out well.

"Good. He will be most pleased to hear this news, especially since the lost Parthian eagles and standards have now been returned to him after so many years held by our enemy in the East. I need not tell you it would go very badly with you if you lost your own legionary eagle to barbarians. Especially now."

"You need not tell me that, and do not tell Caesar how close we came to defeat here," Lollius replied, in what was almost a pleading tone, sighing deeply. Then he nodded, knowing these men would tell Caesar whatever they wanted to tell him and he had no control over their words, "But remember this—we won out at the end of the day and that is all that matters. Rome won decisively and the Germans retreated and sued for peace, and as a price of that peace, they returned our eagle. The problem is solved. Ended."

The Sicillian nodded, as though he accepted the story out of whole cloth, but he did it only for show. He looked at the Greek to see what he would say on the matter.

"Caesar will be most gratified to hear that," Apollodorous told the legate with a slight smile as if all were well now. Then he asked the legate, "My young friend and I have ridden hard and long to get here so quickly. May we have quarters to rest and sleep before we begin our journey back to Rome at dawn? Caesar will want to hear this good news immediately."

"Of course," and the legate had his Centurion of the guard order two of his men to escort the two travelers to a large tent, one that was set aside for legion guests or high ranking officers. Inside were comfortable beds, and a table piled with food and jars of wine.

Once alone in their tent, the Greek spoke up in a confidential tone, "This Marcus Lollius is a fool. He not only lost his eagle, he nearly lost his legion."

"What do you think he is about?" The Sicillian asked thoughtfully. He was curious about the legate. Was he a traitor? Or merely, a fool as the Greek thought? Or just unlucky—and then very lucky?

"I do not know the truth of this, but I like it not, this entire affair troubles me, Rufus."

"Me as well. From what I know of these Germans, they would never just give up a captured eagle, even if what Lollius says is true about him bringing up reinforcements and defeating the enemy here in Gaul. I hear these Germans do not accept defeat so easily."

"Perhaps Lollius is a budding Julius or Agrippa when it comes to fighting?" the Greek asked with a slight laugh.

"You do not really believe that, do you?"

"No, I do not."

"I know, and it makes me wonder."

"Wonder? Yes, I believe something is up and I do not like it," the Greek said allowing his suspicion to show fully now.

"But what?" The Sicillian asked sharply.

The Greek shrugged, "I do not know. Damned if I can see it."

"I have a feeling it may show it's ugly head soon," The Sicillian added, then yawned, shrugged, yawned some more. He was beat. Both men were exhausted from their long hard ride here, and they would begin another long hard ride early on the morrow. "Let us get a few hours of sleep and worry about these matters in the warm clear sun of the morning."

"Agreed," the Greek said, he was already laying in his bed, a well appointed army cot used for officers.

"I will tell you this, that legate is one very lucky fellow. He acted swiftly, attacked boldly, and was victorious," Apollodorous spoke up as the two men made ready to sleep. They each had an army cot, a couple of blankets, nothing luxurious, but certainly luxurious by the standards of traveling out in the open air for many days as they had done so recently.

The Sicillian nodded, stretched, "And he got his eagle back on his own. That saves us a lot of trouble."

"It certainly does, my young friend. Now we may sleep well tonight and then report good news to Caesar when we reach Rome. Caesar likes to hear good news."

"Yes, and truth be told, there is much good news to tell," The Sicillian spoke up in a drowsy voice. "He has the Parthian eagles and standards returned to Rome without war—without one single battle waged, nor one Roman soldier killed—that is quite an accomplishment."

"We did well, my lad," the Greek told his companion as he drifted off to sleep, "and it would not have happened without you. I am sure Caesar will be most pleased. There may even be some reward in it for us. Now let us get some sleep and have sweet dreams of laurels and triumphal rewards."

The night was dark, the moon covered by the clouds, but neither the Greek, nor the Roman could sleep.

"What troubles you, my friend?" Apollodorous finally asked.

"These barbarians, they lost a battle and then returned the eagle. It does not make sense to me," The Sicillian stated grimly.

"I agree. Then what?"

"I do not know," Rufus replied perplexed, then he nodded, looked at his older companion and exclaimed, "By Romulus and Remus! It was a ruse! They set up Lollius, to make him believe he was victorious!"

"So you think…? What are you saying?"

"I think they are going to attack! Tonight! Maybe even now!"

The Greek looked at his young companion most carefully, then nodded, "Wily barbarians for sure. I wonder that I did not see it. I think you may be right, Rufus."

"We must alert the camp right away! The legate!"

The two fighters were still dressed, so tired had they been that they just fell into their cots fully clothed. Now with renewed energy and cold fear, they grabbed their weapons and ran out of the tent into the pitch black night.

"Were are the sentries?" The Greek asked.

"Where are the guards!" The Sicillian shouted.

"Sound the alarm, Rufus! I will alert the legate."

Then the two men rushed off to wake up the camp and roust the guard—and the entire legion.

Moments later the alarms sounded, trumpets blared and drums banged loudly, and the men of *Legio V Alaudae* quickly formed up into their centuries and cohorts and presented themselves ready for battle. They were a fierce looking bunch. They had to be because the barbarians were just as fierce and they were now seen to be swarming into the camp by the dozens, and eventually, by the hundreds!

Full battle struck the legion bare moments later when a horde of screaming wild German barbarians rushed the walls, bounding over the barrier and then struck the men of the legion. The men moved to meet them. The Germans struck at the various formed up centuries—but the Roman soldiers were now ready for the horde, having been alerted. They made a rigid shield wall that held off the attackers—for the moment.

Rufus and Apollodorous were with Legate Lollius and his staff commanding the camp defenses. The legion's perimeter and wall still held in most places, but it had been breached in other areas. Centuries had to be moved quickly to fill in the gaps, even as hundreds of wild and woolly barbarians climbed over the wall and made for the lines of Roman soldiers in a mad rush of shouting bold attackers.

The battle raged on as more barbarians joined their brothers, and it grew as more legionnaires formed up their centuries under the vine canes of stern centurions, though the men needed no such impetus to form up and fight. For all there knew they were in a fight for their life! If they did not win here tonight—there would be no tomorrow morning for the men of this legion. A night battle such as this one was very difficult, the darkness made it possible to make many mistakes. While there were lighted fires that made some vision possible, it was the toughest of battles—a night battle could go either way and no one could control the outcome. The Roman's knew this and made their plans accordingly.

"Form up!" a centurion shouted, and his men rushed to comply with his demand. "Keep order!"

"Shields up!" another centurion shouted to his men and then he ordered them to march forward to meet the rushing barbarians that had climbed over the wall and broken into the plaza of the camp. The battle raged as men from the two sides clashed.

The two sides were further bolstered by more men to join their ranks; more barbarians and more legionnaires. More centuries were marched into position. They were met by mad charges of barbarian Germans. The shield wall was expanded and deepened from one row, eventually to five rows. That put the advantage with the Romans. The men of the legion fought like fury—fighting for their very lives. For they knew that if they were not victorious here this night, they would not be alive when the sun came up. The men of Germania continued to come on like maddened bulls swinging all kinds of deadly sharp swords, pikes, javelins, and any implement that could kill an enemy.

Many of them waved huge battle axes, terrible weapons held by monstrously tall men that dwarfed most of the common Roman soldiers in body size. They shouted and cried out like bloody demons, and against less well-trained troops than the Romans, the battle cries of the barbarians would have had a significant effect. While the screams and cries did unnerve the Romans to some degree, they had been up against these type of opponents in battle before, so it did not interfere with their duty and training. That training bound them solid. They held their ground, and then slowly, advanced.

The battle raged on, but the warning given to the legion by The Sicillian and Apollodorous made all the difference in the outcome. The barbarians thought to have an easy, night battle, a victory won by stealth and surprise. They had not expected the Roman legion to assemble so quickly—almost as if it were ready and waiting for them!

The Romans were not taken unawares by the German attack, as had been the plan. Not totally. That made all the difference. The legion was able to rebound. The Romans had been able to quickly form up their ranks and send their centuries and cohorts to the proper positions to forestall the barbarian attack. And while the barbarians came on hard and fast at the defenders, it was obvious that after an hour of rough and tumble fighting, the Romans were turning the tide and their line was advancing upon the attackers and cutting them down by the hundreds.

"They are spent now!" Lollius shouted to his men, tasting victory, he shouted in rage, "cut them down! Advance *Legio V Alaudae*! Advance and cut them down!"

The legate's words were heard and repeated in dozens of loud vicious shouts by enraged centurions, then acted upon by the men as the legion moved up and the various centuries began to close in on the attackers. In a few moments they had the barbarians in a box—a kill box—and the centuries were moving forward to crush them all in the maw of bloody *pilum* javelins and *gladius* short swords. The fight was closing in on the attackers, and they were growing fatigued and being cut down with almost mechanical Roman precision. The Roman death machine cut down the enemy like a scythe cutting wheat.

"Surrender! Surrender now, or die!" the Legate shouted his demand, and that cry was taken up by the men of the legion against the remaining barbarians.

The Germans ignored the request, and only fought back all the harder as most barbarous peoples were prone to do against the men of

Rome. It would prove a big mistake and their undoing. Their resistance was to no avail however, for now the Germans were trapped in a kill box and they knew it. Their plan of surprise attack had failed. Their leader had figured well on the arrogance and stupidity of Legate Lollius, but he had not figured that a Greek and a Sicillian newly come into the Roman camp would see through the ruse of his returning the eagle—to make it appear his fighting force was no longer a threat. It had been a good plan, but by the gods, it had not worked.

"Kill them, or take them as slaves! Kill the wounded!" one of the centurions ordered his men, and the order was taken to heart by the men who moments before were fighting for their very life in a surprise attack, and now wanted revenge. They took it.

"Bloody mess," The Sicillian said to the Greek as they fought off the few remaining enemy. There was now a brief pause, room to breathe, even talk.

"Yes, but necessary, they must be taught a lesson," Apollodorous replied, cleaning his sword upon the fur cape of a down and bleeding German warrior he had just slain. "That was too damn close! They almost had us, Rufus. They almost had the entire legion caught in a surprise attack that would have doomed us all—and then they would get the eagle as well. Caesar would be enraged had the legate lost this battle. I have no idea what he would have done for punishment to the legate and the legion, perhaps even decimation of the survivors?"

"Had we lost this battle, Greek, there would be no survivors," The Sicillian replied.

"Yes, of course, you are correct."

"Well, I am just thankful we saw through that damnable ruse and were able to alert the legion in time. At least the legate took our warning to heart."

"*Our* warning? *You* figured it out, lad. You saved the legion!"

The Sicillian shook his head as he wiped his sweating blood-splattered face, both men were exhausted, covered in the blood of their enemy, and some of their own, as were all of the lucky and blessed survivors of the legion were this night. It had been a hard fought fight, in less than two hours of intense battle in the mostly dark of night, hundreds of barbarians had been put to death and dozens of legionnaires had meet their doom to wander the fields of Elysium forever. It had been a hard fought, hard won battle.

As the bloody night ended, and the sun came up in Roman Gaul, the last of the German barbarian invaders were being rounded up and chained in long columns, to be sold as slaves. Or to go to Rome to be fodder for the Games. The enemy wounded were being silenced, with a quick sword stroke. The Roman wounded received better treatment, they were being picked up and taken care of by their comrades, and the few Greek healers who were assigned to the legion for medical purposes. The remaining men of *Legio V Alaudae* let out with a wild ground-shaking cheer of victory when the legate pronounced they had been victorious in a great battle.

The Sicillian and the Greek just grinned at each other, thankful they were still alive, knowing the Fates had been with them that night. For it had indeed been a close run thing.

CHAPTER: XIIII

After the attack and defeat of the German barbarians in Gaul, and receiving the valued thanks of Legate Lollius and the men of the *Legio V Alaudae*, the ride to Rome for The Sicillian and his Greek mentor was blessedly uneventful.

Uneventful, except for the attack the two men were forced to encounter at the northern fringe of the Appian Way as they made their way south into *Italia* and towards the city of *Roma*. It was there that a group of brigands accosted them. There were four of them, well-built, and well-armed. Certainly former military men, perhaps deserters? Former gladiators? Perhaps even Praetorians? Who could be sure these days.

The four were awaiting them at the crossroads that met with the Appian Way that led south into Italia. They were well horsed and held drawn swords. Their was no doubt about what they were about.

The Greek spoke up when he saw the men and instantly knew what they were about, "The only thing I wonder, my youthful friend, is if someone told these men in advance where to meet us. It was no secret we were riding south this morning, riding to Rome. Someone, perhaps, from *Legio V Alaudae* even, may have given us away?"

"I hope you are wrong, Apollodorous," The Sicillian replied, that meant a traitor in the legion. It was not something Rufus wanted to think about now. For now, both men drew their swords, ready for the attack that was coming, as the four riders charged down the road at them with horses racing at full run and wicked shiny swords held high in the morning sun. There was no talk this time, no questions, no pretense of these men being brigands or thieves.

"Have a care, these four are out for a quick sure kill."

"Yes, I see it, they are all about grim business. But so are we," The Sicillian answered as he drove his mount into the pack of four approaching riders. The Greek was at his side, swinging his sword like a demon and quickly cut down first one attacker, and then quickly engaged another of the enemy. It was obvious these men did not count on the finely trained fighting ability of the Roman and Greek they thought to so easily take down and kill. The fight raged on with clashing swords, snorting horses screaming in anger and pain, and cursing men as blood was sprayed from terrible wounds.

"I am two ahead of you, Rufus," the Greek chided loudly at his companion in gory glory, as he had just dispatched his second attacker down to Hades. "Did you not learn anything from me about how to prevail in a close-in fight?"

"You shall see what I have learned soon enough, Greek!" The Sicillian shouted back grimly, moving at the remaining two riders, who were trying to outflank him. He was not going to allow that. The Sicillian moved his warhorse easily around into a good position, then he took a jab with his *gladius* at the rider on his left. He hit his target with a swift sureness and dug his sword deeply into the man's vitals. Then he drew back and turned swiftly as he slashed wildly at the other man who he knew would be coming upon him to take advantage of his attack on the man he had just downed. Rufus quickly moved close, then slid his sword blade across that man's open throat. Blood gushed out in mighty spurts and the man fell from his horse to the cold stone cobbles of the Appian Way. The four men now lay dead at their feet. The victor looked over the bodies of the vanquished for any evidence of who these men were, or who they worked for, but there was nothing. They examined them and their goods carefully. There was no evidence. It was exasperating.

"Round up their horses, we will take them with us," the Greek told his companion. "We can always sell them."

The Sicillian nodded and rounded up the horses of the four men they had just slain.

"They thought to take us easily because they outnumbered us and would attack us first and fast, but they did not think it would be *us* who would attack *them*!" the Greek said with pride.

The Sicillian smiled wryly, "We were lucky, Greek, we were lucky, and the Fates were with us this day, as they were with us and the legion last night."

"Then we are truly blessed, Rufus," the Greek responded with a grim laugh.

"You think so?" The Sicillian replied dubiously.

"No. But whatever the reason, I am happy at the result. Now let us get to Rome and Caesar, we have dawdled here long enough!"

"One question?" Rufus asked his companion curiously.

"Only one? My, my, you are indeed maturing. So what is it?"

"Who are they, and why do they want to kill us?"

"That is two questions, my friend."

"Two then. What do you think about this?"

"Truly, I do not know. We have found no evidence or papers to go by as to answer any of your questions. They may be former legionaries," Apollodorous told his young friend as they looked back at the four dead bodies of the men they had just killed. They were left there, where they lay, upon the stones of the Appian Way to serve as a marker to others who might try their swords against them. "Or something else."

The Sicillian nodded but grew wary, "Could these men be Praetorians?" He thought back upon his actions with Milo and his band of Praetorians—dressed under cover as simple travelers—who had come upon him last year. They had been out to kill him. And there were others he had met on the road in the service of Caesar, who had tried to kill him—also the Greek. Were these men of that ilk? Or were they Liberators? Remnants of the men who supported the murder of the Devine Julius? And if so, who had sent them, and why? He could not figure it out yet, but he knew that one day he would and on that day he would make some arrangements with his *gladius* upon his enemy.

The Sicillian knew that he and his Greek mentor were not so important as to need assassination by such special methods of subterfuge or attack, but already attempts had been made. Why? Even back in Armenia, in the very palace of King Tigranes, the assassin Mardus had come at Rufus. He spoke of some of that now with Apollodorous.

His Greek friend was not surprised by the admission.

"Who can say, Rufus. There is much political subterfuge going on behind the scenes in every nation these days, and in every province of the Empire. Each governor sees himself as the next Consul, or the next Caesar, but they are careful in their words and actions. Very careful. Caesar Augustus rules and all seems stable and content for the time being, but I fear that under the surface the Empire roils and boils like Mount Aetna itself."

"I agree, but what of these plotters?"

"There are plotters everywhere these days, my friend. Let us not worry overmuch about them for now. Come, let us ride on, and talk no more of it for now, Caesar is expecting us in Rome and we must make all haste to get there and attend him. We have much to report and I know he is anxious to hear it all."

CHAPTER XV

Once in Rome the two weary riders were immediately escorted into the imperial palace upon the Palentine Hill. It was not called the palace by those in Rome, and certainly not by Caesar, but it was the imperial place all the same—the home of the emperor—also a word and a title Augustus forbid anyone to use regarding him. He was known as Caesar, which was his family name, or simply as The *Princeps*. The First Citizen. Nevertheless, his home was a magnificent structure worthy of an emperor, white stone, gleaming marble, Caesar's elite German guards escorted the two travelers through the place and into his presence. The two travelers looked at these giants with some interest and trepidation as they had just a day ago fought some similar barbarians, but Caesar's German Guard were entirely trustworthy, being of a different tribe. They all had taken a blood oath and were totally loyal to Caesar—as where they. Soon the two travelers were brought into the presence of the ruler of the world.

Caesar Augustus was alone and welcomed his two guests graciously.

"Rufus! And Apollodorous, you old dog! So good to see you both. And both alive and none the worse for wear, I can see," Caesar told them in a buoyant tone. He hugged the two men, shook their forearms in the Roman fashion and then personally poured them each a drink of blood red wine in a golden goblet. It was a most generous gesture of welcome that was not lost upon the two men. Caesar was obviously grateful to them for the success in their recent missions.

"Thank you, Caesar, and it is good to see you well and in such high spirits," the Greek replied with a wide grin as he gulped the delicious wine. Both men were very thirsty and the cool wine, diluted with water, was most welcome.

The Sicillian also smiled, nodded agreeably, but remained silent for the moment as he enjoyed the happy reunion and the drink.

"And why not express my joy! The Parthians have returned my eagles and standards lost by those fools Crassus and Antony, and regained by myself—with your help, of course. And that fool of a legate,

Marcus Lollius has saved the honor of my *Legio V Alaudae* by regaining his lost eagle in battle. He did regain it, did he not?"

"Yes, Caesar," the Greek replied quickly.

"So you know all about that?" The Sicillian spoke up carefully. He wondered just what Caesar knew, or how much he had been told. It was good that Rufus and his friend now would not have to keep the secret—now that it was out. Caesar did not like to have any news kept from him. Good news—or especially bad news.

"Yes, I need not your report on the matter in Roman Gaul, my spies are everywhere, they tell me things. You two did very well in the East, by the way. Those damnable Parthians—I almost set Agrippa loose on them—just to teach them a lesson. He was eager, let me tell you. I had the devil of a time holding him back, but then I decided against it. We do not need the turmoil of another major war at this time. It would not be wise. So that is settled, at least for now. Do you know what I am going to do now?"

The two visitors looked at each other a bit ominously, and then back to Caesar with questioning looks, neither had any clue as to what the great man meant now, or what he might say or do next.

Caesar finally smiled and spoke up firmly, "Well, tomorrow we are going to have a triumph through the Forum and the entire city, celebrating my return of the eagles and standards back to the warm bosom of Rome. You both were instrumental in this success. Therefore, I want you both to ride in my chariot with me to enjoy this victory."

Caesar Victorious!

Roma Victor!

Augustus the undefeated!

Augustus the Conqueror!

Apollodorous smiled and nodded eagerly, "Of course, Caesar, nothing would make us happier."

"That is most generous of you, Caesar," The Sicillian added, and meant it. It was a high honor to lavish upon two men who were not of any noble blood.

"Nonsense, I would never have had this bloodless victory without your help and I do want you to know I appreciate your efforts for Rome—and on my behalf. I want you both to know that, and to reap the reward of it. Here, look at these."

Caesar Augustus allowed a wide grin and handed Rufus and Apollodorous each what looked like to be newly minted silver *sesterces*.

"Look at them! Are they not lovely?" Caesar said with outward joy.

The two men looked at the silver coins carefully. They were indeed newly minted and shone brightly. Upon one side were pressed images of Roman legionary eagles and standards, while upon the other side of the coin were the words "*Signis receptis*", which was denoting the return of the legions icons and detailing honors awarded to Caesar Augustus from the Senate. Which he had, by the way, most humbly refused. He always refused such honors, even as he increased his power and influence.

"You see, all is well now, my friends, and on the morrow, you shall both ride with me in the victory procession," Caesar slapped both men jovially upon the back. He was in high spirits this day and proud of how this mission had turned out. It was a plan that had turned out far better than even he had imagined. "Never again while I am in command shall a legion lose it's eagle! I forbid it!"

"Yes, Caesar," the Greek spoke up quickly. Hopefully.

"Now go, enjoy your stay in Rome. I will see you both on the morrow, early. After the ceremony, I shall reward you each with a presentation of these newly minted silver coins. You shall both be wealthy men, but it is nothing less than you deserve. I thank you both, once again. Now you may take your leave."

"Thank you, Caesar," The Sicillian spoke up as he made ready to leave the chamber.

"Most generous of you, my lord," the Greek chimed in with a wide bow that included a grin of sheer joy and relief that things had gone so well. Almost too well. It was almost too much to believe. Surely the gods smiled down upon them all this day.

"Oh, one more thing. Rufus, before you go," Caesar spoke up as if he had just remembered something of importance. "My sister, Octavia, is here in Rome, newly arrived, and she wishes to speak to you. You know, she confided in me that she was quite worried for your safety, but I assured her that you would win through, just as you always do. Regardless, she would like to see you now, and then after the festivities tomorrow, I have a new mission for you and Apollodorous to take on for me. Something most interesting, I can assure you. If you are willing?"

The two men looked carefully at each other. There was nothing else to say but to accept Caesar's request.

"Of course, Caesar!" The Sicillian spoke up firmly, offering a stern salute, copied by the Greek as well.

"We would be most happy to take on any mission you have for us," the Greek replied carefully. It was the wise response. Details could be gotten later, and at this point, he did not want to even hear them. Who knew what Caesar had in that devious mind of his? The Greek sighed, he knew he and his young partner would find out about it all soon enough. Until then, enjoy the triumph tomorrow, and accept Caesar's gift of the newly minted silver coins. After all, it was nothing more than they deserved.

Caesar told the two men, but focused his eyes upon The Sicillian, "Good, my friends, that is what I like to see, then go now to see my sister, Rufus, and allay her fear for your health. You know, we both worry for your safety."

"I know that, Caesar, and I thank you both for your concern for my welfare."

CHAPTER: XVI

"We have so little time, my love," Lady Octavia spoke in haste to the young Sicillian warrior who had come to her personal chambers located in a special wing of the imperial palace. There were spies and eyes everywhere so the two lovers must remain circumspect in their personal meetings, but even so their love and passion crept into their feelings when they looked upon each other. It was in their eyes, their lips, their heated embraces.

"You have been gone so long," Octavia told her younger lover as they held each other tightly, as if they never wanted to let go of each other.

"Not so long, I am back now."

"Yes, back here in Rome, but for how long a time?"

"Not for long, I am afraid. Your brother spoke to Apollodorous and myself about another mission, something he wants us to undertake for him after the triumph and ceremony tomorrow," Rufus told her in a soft tone.

The Lady Octavia looked angry but said nothing.

The Sicillian just smiled, such was life in Rome these days, for they each served Rome—and by extension Caesar—each in their own ways.

"Be careful my darling, there is danger lurking behind every column and on every street here in Rome."

"I am aware of the dangers, but it is all worth it to see you again, to hold you, to kiss you," he told her, stroking her long curly ringlets. While she was older than him by some years, her youthful looks and demeanor, made her appear to be much younger. It was a trait of the Julians that Augustus and his sister shared. Both appeared to be many years younger in age than they actually were.

"It is good news about the return of the eagles and standards. Is it not? My brother is overjoyed by your part in it," Octavia told Rufus allowing her enthusiasm to show. "You did well. He will reward you well."

"Yes, so he told me, and then after the ceremony he will send Apollodorous and I out once more upon some new deadly mission. But that is well. I am not complaining, only that it will keep us apart. I am happy to be here and see you now, to spend what little time we have left, together. Short as it must be."

"The night is still young, my brave Sicillian," she told him in a husky voice as her lips brushed against his own. Then she held them there for a prolonged deep kiss.

Rufus smiled, "That it is. And do you want company this evening?"

"I always want your company, my love. Come with me, I have a chamber in the other wing of the palace where we may spend the night together. Undisturbed."

"But if your brother finds out about us, it will go badly for you," Rufus spoke up, which was true enough, and it would also go even worse for him, but he did not mention that for he did not care about himself, only his Lady Octavia. He just did not want his Lady Octavia to be placed in any untenable situation with her brother. That could lead to trouble, even exile.

"Fear not, my love. We are safe for the evening. The servants and slaves are all gone, sent out for the night. All has been planned and is in readiness for our private moment tonight."

Gaetano Salvidienus Rufus smiled, kissed the Lady Octavia and followed her to their special room.

CHAPTER: XVII

The night passed much too quickly and the next morning came too soon.

Rufus and Apollodorous met Caesar at the appointed time and place, and then the ceremonial procession commemorating the triumphant return of the legions eagles and standards from the Parthian wars was underway. It was a massive procession through the heart of Rome, and through the Forum, ringed by lines of stout Praetorians in polished armor and spotless white tunics and cloaks, lined the way on either side, and the people were out in the tens and hundreds of thousands cheering and joyful.

As promised, The Sicillian and Apollodorous stood beside Caesar Augustus in his own personal chariot. The honored first in line, behind the lead chariot that displayed the returned eagles and standards. The legions icons were displayed in the lead chariot for all the people to see and bask in the victory. The cheers when these icons passed them were ear-splittingly loud. Lady Octavia rode in the third chariot behind Caesar. The Lady Livia, Caesar's wife, was not present on this occasion.

Caesar basked in the glory and applause and wild cheers of the populace. He waved grandly to the crowds who cheered him ever more. At one point it seemed the people actually cheered Caesar more than they cheered the returned eagles—and The Sicillian was sure that Caesar wanted it to be that way. Then Caesar looked upon him in a most thoughtful manner. What now, the young warrior thought.

"You saw my sister last evening," Caesar told The Sicillian as they rode through the cheering throngs of the Forum of Rome. The eagles and standards rode in colorful displays in the brightly decorated chariot in front of Caesar. In front of that chariot marched a full cohort of Praetorian guardsmen, marching in rhythm to the beat of heavy pounding drums that sounded out a powerful cadence. Trumpets blared loudly. It was a most impressive spectacle, even by Roman standards.

The Sicillian looked carefully at Caesar, a bit uncertain how to respond to his words. For his words had not been a question, but a statement, which meant he knew—something. It had certainly seemed to be a loaded statement. Or did the youth just feel some pang of guilt about his secret liaison with Octavia, with the two of them going behind her brother's back? The Sicillian played it simple and stoic for the moment, he nodded simply, then added, "Yes, I saw her."

"That is good, she was most concerned for your safety—as was I."

The Sicillian spoke not another word. Apollodorous, who was close-by in the same chariot, said not one word either. A woman of quality such as the Lady Octavia was not for one such as The Sicillian.

Then Caesar Augustus looked straight into the eyes of Rufus and said with total assurance, "Of course, *you* know that *I* know, Rufus."

It was not a question, it was a statement of complete assurance.

And that was all that Great Caesar said, but it was enough.

The Sicillian gulped nervously, but said nothing. There was nothing to say. Apollodorous looked nervous. At any moment Caesar could call for a death sentence upon the young Sicillian lad, but Caesar spoke not a word. He seemed to be keeping his true intentions unknown—for now. No ranks of armed praetorians were called by Caesar to the chariot.

The procession advanced onwards through the Forum, snaking through the wide avenues and boulevards of the city. The cheers for Caesar growing louder. The people of Rome were ecstatic at this bold bloodless victory. Caesar had reclaimed the honors lost by Crassus and Antony. Caesar had proven to all that he was superior even to Crassus and Antony. Caesar was in a very good mood that day and he knew who to thank for his good fortune.

The ruler of the civilized world looked closely at The Sicillian with his sharp and penetrating eyes, "You, Gaetano Salvidienus Rufus, have always been my good loyal friend and have served me well, even as had your father."

The Sicillian only nodded. He did not know what to say, or what to expect.

The Greek stood by concerned, but knew to remain silent for the moment. He needed to gauge which way this particular wind was blowing.

Caesar nodded sagely, then continued, "But you are a soldier, not a noble, not a prince, or king, and as such you can not marry my sister, the Lady Octavia. You do understand that, do you not?"

"Yes, Caesar, of course," The Sicillian replied nervously, for now he, and the Greek standing beside him in the chariot of honor, knew that Caesar knew about the affair between Rufus and his sister, the Lady Octavia.

Then Caesar allowed a thin smile that set both men concerned and perplexed. "My dear sister has had two husbands already, one was the cur Marc Antony, my doing of course, but it had to be done to avert civil war at the time. I do love her, no matter what the scribes may say, or what the Senators murmur. I want her to have her happiness, but also she must to do her duty to Rome. Do you understand?"

"I am afraid I do not understand these complicated political matters, Caesar," Rufus spoke up, while Apollodorous gave him a slight nudge to remind him to be very careful now with his words.

"Her duty to Rome—and myself—means that at some time she must become a member of a suitably arranged marriage. Allying the Julians to another powerful family. You do understand that?"

The Sicillian did not reply.

The Greek spoke up then, "Of course he does, Caesar."

Caesar ignored the Greek and looked intently at young Rufus.

"You do understand that?" Caesar repeated. He did not like to repeat himself, ever, but under the circumstances, he allowed it. He could see how nervous his young friend was, and with good reason, but he did not have any truey animus towards The Sicillian. Quite the contrary, in fact.

Rufus quickly nodded, he understood what Caesar had told him only too well.

"Good, then that is now all settled and clearly understood. However, in the meantime, before that happens, and the time may never even come for such an arranged marriage, my sister's happiness is my main concern. If she can be happy with you, Rufus, even for a little while, then I will not stand in the way of you two keeping company with each other. But under no conditions, will there be any marriage, or even a thought of marriage or any legal binding. You understand? But putting all that aside, see her as you will and enjoy the love you two have for each other. Life and love can be so fleeting, it is precious. I know."

The Sicillian let out a deep breath of relief.

Gaetano Salvidienous Rufus could not believe what he was hearing. It was quite amazing, and not what he expected at all. He was being given permission to court Caesar's sister, all unofficial of course, but it was still most welcome, and no one need die because of it, "Surely, Caesar, of course, and…thank you."

"Surely, my old friend," Caesar Augustus told Rufus with a light smile, then he grasped his arm in the Roman manner and the two men hugged as the crowd cheered, and the procession of gilded chariots pulled by caparisoned horses moved onward through the streets of Rome.

Apollodorous let out a great sigh of relief, and The Sicillian looked over at the lovely young woman in the chariot behind his own and smiled with pure joy, as she smiled back at him.

"Are you happy now, Rufus?" Caesar asked The Sicillian a moment later.

"More than I could ever express to you, My Lord, and I thank you for your understanding in the matter."

"Do not thank me, I do it for Octavia, but I am delighted that if it be anyone, that you are her paramour, for you are a good friend and a valued one, to us both. You are a good man as well, who I am sure will treat her well."

"Of course, certainly, and I thank you, Caesar," Rufus whispered softly. He was brimming over with happiness at this good news. At this somewhat, partial, acceptance of his love of Octavia by her brother. He hardly saw the crowd or heard their loud cheering now as the procession continued to move onwards throughout the city of Rome. It was a magical city to him this day, a city where anything might be possible. He knew, it was an unrealistic view, but he savored it for the moment. He only thought of the fact that he was now able to visit Octavia and be with her openly, or at least openly but discreetly, and not having a death sentence over their heads should Caesar find out about their relationship. The truth was out now, and Caesar was accepting of it—for the moment. A reward to him, no doubt, for his work in Parthia. Perhaps? The reason did not really matter to him now. He was full of joy and the world seemed like a special place, and he cared not what tomorrow might bring.

"I am delighted you are pleased, Rufus," Caesar told him suddenly, breaking in on his pleasant thoughts, "for tomorrow you and Apollodorous will leave upon your most dangerous mission for me and Rome. I know that you both shall serve me and Rome as well as always."

"Always, Caesar!" The Sicillian replied firmly.

"Our word is our bond, Mighty Caesar!" the Greek added sternly. Serious.

Caesar Augustus nodded, then he looked away and waved again to the cheering crowd, reveling in the adoration, but never fooled by it. For he was not the son of the Devine Julius for nothing, and he never forgot that fact.

The triumphant procession moved on through the broad avenues and byways of Greater Rome. The Sicillian thought of the time to come with Octavia and the fact that they could now keep company together openly. It was glorious, precious, something to look forward to with every fiber of his being.

Apollodorous, ever the wily Greek thinker, allowed some of his Athenian cynicism to enter his thoughts. He was happy for his young friend, and for the Lady Octavia who he truly admired, but he had his concerns. The two were playing a dangerous game now that their love for each other was known to Caesar. It seemed not to matter to the ruler of the world, but the Greek wondered about what the result of it all would be. Surely not something very good. Meanwhile, the Greek also wondered what this new and deadly mission might entail? Surely nothing easy or safe. Such missions for Caesar were certain to always be highly dangerous, and yet, was this mission something else? Perhaps something more?

The Greek wondered about it. Might this new mission be some way for Caesar to get rid of an annoying problem? For the Greek knew that Caesar was a master at eliminating problems, and it seemed that his young Sicillian friend had now become a problem to mighty Caesar. It was possible. Or perhaps not? Caesar, if nothing else while being enigmatic—he could have been a Greek, and in fact had been tutored by Greek scholars, such as Apollodorous—was extremely loyal to those who served him faithfully. No one served Caesar more loyally and with such devotion as The Sicillian—unless it be the General Agrippa. Caesar would not go against any man who was loyal to him—and no man was more loyal to Caesar than The Sicillian. The Greek shook his head, trying to understand and work it all out. What did it mean? Perhaps things were just not as they appeared to be? Perhaps? There was much to think about here. Much to think about while they were on the road to who knew where, and what new mission, in the vastness of the Great Roman Empire?

The Greek was perplexed. And there was something else that was bothering him. Who were the assassins that had plagued Rufus in Gaul, and later in Armenia, and lately both of them upon the Appian Way?

Liberators? Agents of an enemy? Surely, but which enemy? Or were they sent by someone closer, more trusted, perhaps even by Great Caesar himself? He did not want to contemplate that dire possibility.

Apollodorous the Greek was happy that his young friend, Rufus, could now openly spend time with the woman he loved, he just wondered what danger would come next. There was always some new danger on the horizon. But he knew, that whatever it might be, The Sicillian and he would be ready for it and meet it together.

CHAPTER: XVIII

"My love, my darling," the Lady Octavia asked the slim young man who lay in bed beside her, "you are troubled?"

"No, just thinking. Time is short, it is so fleeting and goes by so quickly. I must leave you soon. Caesar requires the Greek and myself to embark upon a new mission for him, we leave Rome once the sun comes up."

"That is but a couple of hours from now," the lovely woman said with disappointment, noting the darkness of the night was still apparent. "I thought Augustus told you he knew about our liaison and accepted it."

"Accepted it—for now, my love."

"So you must go so soon?"

"He requires it," The Sicillian said simply. Both knew that Caesar's word was law—for good or ill. Rufus had to make himself ready.

"I know, so then let us make the best of the little time that we have left together."

The Sicillian smiled, held the Lady Octavia tightly and kissed her hard, she was like honey in his arms, warm, and tantalizing. The fragrance of her hair was enticing.

"So where to next?" she asked him trying to hold back her concern for his welfare. "Or is it a state secret? My brother is so full of secrets these days."

"I do not know, Caesar has not yet told me, nor has he told the Greek. That in itself is odd. We are to meet with him before dawn, before the sun comes up, and then he will personally give us our orders."

The Lady Octavia shook her head ominously, "Such secrecy, so mysterious, even unto the last moment of your leaving? That is not good, my love, be watchful of daggers in the back."

The Sicillian smiled boldly, "I am aware of the dangers, my love, and of the benefits, when I come back to you once this mission is over and done with."

"Yes, think upon those benefit's my love in your darkest hours. In the meantime, see that you do come back to me, Gaetano," the Lady

Octavia told him with a warm embrace calling him by his first name in a soft tone. "Come back to me, and I shall await your return."

"I shall come back to you, if I have to wade through dark Hades to do so."

"You may have to do just that, my love," she warned him.

The Sicillian smiled grimly, he knew she was not exaggerating, even as he wondered just what new mischief Caesar had in mind for him and his Greek companion now. He whispered, "I know that, but I shall do it gladly to be back once again at your side where I belong."

"Keep yourself alive, my darling," she told him with a kiss, as he got up to leave her.

"I always endeavor to do so, my love," he replied with a boyish grin, and then he was gone. Gone to find the Greek, and then the two rushed to meet secretly with Caesar Augustus in the other wing of the palace in his private suite of rooms.

The Sicillian wondered just what was to come next, but he knew that such last moment secrecy from Caesar himself, meant that it might prove his most dangerous and deadly mission yet. He nodded, accepting of his role, as he took a last, loving look at the Lady Octavia, even as she watched him take his leave of her, he nodded grimly and whispered softly, "For Caesar—and Rome!"

CHAPTER: XIX

"You are late!" Apollodorous said as he met up with Rufus in a hallway in the central wing of the palace.

"I came as soon as I could."

"No doubt, regardless Caesar awaits, we can not be late. You play a dangerous game, my lad, his sister is not for you," the Greek advised him as they trod the hallways of the palace to the special rooms where Caesar Augustus had told them they were to meet him at.

"What do you think he has on his mind?" The Sicillian asked his friend and mentor as they quickly walked down the quiet halls. It seemed strange that there were so few guards on duty.

"Who can tell, the secrecy has me worried, though, it reeks of deadly danger. Perhaps of the type we have never encountered before."

"Always the cheerful fellow in the morning, eh?"

"It is not morning, not yet, so who can say what the day will bring us?"

The two men went on their way, they were ushered through various posted palace guards, all Praetorians who were most steadfast in their protection of Caesar. Finally they were met by one of the major clerks, a respected freedman, who was one of the rare few valued government functionaries who put Caesar's will into action. He quickly ushered the two men into a room saying with obvious annoyance, "He is waiting for you. He has been waiting for you."

Then the man left them and carefully closed the door behind him.

The Sicillian and the Greek found themselves alone now in a large and sumptuous chamber that led into a suite of equally sumptuous rooms. It was a place fit for a king, even though Caesar made it clear at every opportunity that he was not any king. But these two men knew the truth, Augustus was king in everything but name.

"You are late!" a voice was heard in firm tone and Caesar Augustus walked into the room. His body was totally covered in a long regal cape, "sit down."

Rufus and Apollodorous took a seat at a table that was piled high with all manner of exquisite food and drink. It would make a sumptuous feast. However, they did not dare reach for any of the tempting food or drink until Caesar offered them to do so. And as of yet, he had not offered them to do so.

"You know why you are here?"

"Another mission?" the Greek responded simply, curious in tone.

"Because I can trust you both," Caesar replied sternly.

The two men nodded, that much was certainly true. Both men were totally loyal to Caesar and to Rome.

"Yes, Caesar," The Sicilian spoke up.

"Of course, Caesar," the Greek added.

Caesar Augustus nodded, smiled softly, "You have a new mission to undertake for me and I need you both now more than ever. It is the most important mission of your lives, and of my own life as well."

"What is it, Caesar? We will do anything you require, you know that?" the Greek spoke up honestly. He and Augustus went back a long way, as did the relationship between Rufus and Caesar.

"I know that, but this one will prove a might delicate," Caesar began, then walked over to the two men. "You know how I am able to keep Rome strong? You know how I am able to keep Rome, Rome? United and victorious—and at peace."

"The army," the Greek replied. "You control the legions."

The Sicilian nodded, for he knew this was true since the time of the Triumvirate and Marc Antony.

"Yes, that is true, that is the obvious answer, but there are other considerations. Do you know what they are?" Augustus looked intently at the two men before him.

The two men remained silent. Caesar was in his teacher scholarly mode now and would explain it all soon enough. They kept silent, listened, and waited.

Caesar nodded, asked them, "No? Well, it is not often spoken of. It is all about one simple reality—allies. Rome needs allies. Allies in the form of other tribes, outside kingdoms, even if they be barbarian. In some cases, especially if they be barbarian. So what you are going to do is to escort my special representative to meet with a barbarian king and then help him secure that king's aid to fight for Rome. Quite simple, really, do you not think?"

"Simple? It sounds simple, in theory. I know nothing is simple, Caesar, but if you will it, it shall be done," The Sicilian spoke up firmly.

The Greek nodded his head in agreement.

"Good, that is all I can ask of you. Then in one hour you will meet my special representative at the Vespa Gate. Ask no questions when you meet this man. Not one word, do you understand? The three of you will immediately ride northwest towards the Danube River, and the Roman province of Dacia, where a treaty shall be made—or war shall come again to Rome. In the meantime, enjoy the food and drink that I have had prepared for you here."

Then Caesar Augustus was gone.

One hour later The Sicillian and the Greek stood waiting nervously at the Vespa Gate with three strong warhorses. The Sicillian's beloved Batavian steed was one of them.

"No Praetorians around at all," the Greek whispered carefully. That was most odd.

"No guards, no one is here," The Sicillian whispered back, his hand drifting to the hilt of his sword. Was this some kind of ambush? Trap?

Then they heard someone coming silently towards them.

"I am here!" they heard a sudden voice tell them from the shadows. It was a voice they instantly recognized and it belonged to a man who was entirely covered in a dark cape. It was a single man dressed as a common tradesman, his face and features covered by his clothing and cloak.

"I am Caesar's representative. We leave now. Mount up, gentlemen, we have a long ride and much to do," the man ordered.

Apollodorous looked ominously at The Sicillian, "Well, come on lad, a new dawn and a new adventure."

The Sicillian nodded, there was not much to say at that point, the man obviously wanted to leave Rome in secrecy, to of all things, travel to the lands at the Danube to meet with some barbarian king. Something was up and it was very secret and very dangerous, and he wondered why Caesar would send his valued representative to only travel with two trusted men, and not a cohort or two of his vaulted Praetorians at the least, to such a meeting.

However, now both The Sicillian and the Greek realized precisely just who the man was here who represented Caesar—*it was Caesar Augustus himself!*

Caesar Augustus smiled at The Sicillian, and then spoke up softly, "I know you and the Greek must have a thousand questions, and at the proper time I promise that I will make it all clear to you both. For now, accept that we three are on a new mission for Rome, so let us ride like the wind, out of the city and away from *Italia* and to the wild lands north of the Danube. There I shall find the allies Rome needs—or begin a new war that no one wants. Least of all me. Now we ride!"

HISTORICAL NOTE:

Writing a novel *based* on history, but not *actual* history, poses some interesting and significant challenges for any writer. While this is a work of fiction, it is based upon a template built from historical facts and some actual persons who lived during the days of Ancient Rome.

Octavian, was just a slim youth of 18 years in 44 B.C., when Julius Caesar was assassinated on the Ides of March, initiating a long and deadly chain of events that would, after many years and much struggle, leave him as the sole ruler of Rome. And, more importantly, firmly in command of the legions of Rome. For the legions *were* the Roman Empire!

For many historians and novelists (and in popular TV and films), this point in history has become the end of the story. The rise of Octavian; his avenging Julius Caesar's murder; and years later taking down Cleopatra and Mark Antony, have been told over and over. Even a guy named Shakespeare—quite a long while ago—told this story in his play *Julius Caesar*.

However, Octavian's story and the story of the Emperor's of Rome did not end there.

In fact, it was just beginning!

Octavian soon transformed himself into Augustus Caesar—at which point he had become virtual sole ruler of the Western half of the empire for over a decade. After that point, he would go on to rule Rome and the entire empire for *another 43 years!*

This novel begins the story at that point in those later years as they might have been, loosely based on history, but based on history nevertheless—told through the eyes and words of his most important agent—The Sicillian, Gaetano Silvidienus Rufus. This is the story of The Sicillian and his adventures in the service of Caesar Augustus and Rome. Together they form a bond that lasts throughout the years of empire.

Augustus Caesar was a very hands-on ruler, he personally fought in various battles, traveled to all of the Roman provinces. He did not just rule from a throne in Rome as many mistakenly believe. In fact, of his 43 years as *Princeps*, First Citizen of the Empire, he spent most of those years outside of Rome in the provinces. He was a unique ruler who set the template for the empire, and for Roman emperors for a thousand years.

History tells us that for many years Rome was in a deadly struggle to conqueror northern *Hispania*. In the first book in this series, the Cantabrians and Asturians fought what was in effect a guerrilla war against the Roman legions, where they suddenly attacked, and then quickly retreated to the safety of their mountains. They were impossible to defeat that way, and had to be lured out of their mountain strongholds. Eventually they were lured into battle. Augustus finally beat them when they came down from the mountains to fight what they thought to be a weak, and weakly led, Roman legion in a set piece battle. This was a battle on the terms of the legions and one which they won conclusively. The battle was won and the war was over. For now.

In my second novel in the series, *The Sicillian: Book 2: Augustus The Conqueror*, the story is also based upon facts as they occurred during the reign of Caesar Augustus. Twice, Roman armies under Crassus, and then Marc Antony, invaded the eastern rival empire of Parthia with disastrous results. Crassus not only lost seven legions, he was captured and killed by the Parthians by being forced to drink molten gold! So there was mush animosity between Parthia and Rome. The return to Rome of their lost legionary eagles and other standards, as well as surviving prisoners by the Parthians, was one of the most publicized and greatest successes of the reign of Augustus. It came about by diplomacy with Parthia, *not* war. But that did not matter, for it was nevertheless looked upon—and fully publicized by Caesar—as acknowledgement of Roman superiority and victory. Coins were indeed minted by Caesar to commemorate this historic event. So these events did happen, though not exactly as I have depicted them here. Also, though I constrained the timeline by a couple of years, Legate Marcus Lollius of the *Legion V Alaudae* did in fact lose the legion's eagle in battle. The legion broke, after attacks by three German tribes in Roman Gaul and their eagle was indeed, captured. However, before Caesar could go to Gaul with an army to get the eagle back, Lollius won a second battle with the German invaders and recovered his legion's eagle. Lucky fellow!

These books are a lot of fun to write, but they are a lot of work as well. Much research is involved. However, no one who writes such a historical novel does so in a vacuum. There are many fine books and excellent authors whose works have inspired the writing of my Roman books—both non-fiction histories, and fine novels of Roman military adventure fiction. Among the latter I must include the seminal trilogy by Mary Sutcliff; also the rousing military adventure series of novels featuring Marco and Cato by Simon Scarrow. The Ballista novels by Harry Sidebottom are also most excellent, as well as is his non-fiction history works. *The Eagle in The Snow* by Wallace Breem (the basis for the glorious first 20 minutes of the film *Gladiator*), of course, is one of the best military novels about the later Roman Empire, a truly incredible read. All these authors, and many more, imbue Roman military action and adventure with true historical detail and are terrific reads. There are still other novels by other authors that I have not had the pleasure of reading that will be added to this list in future volumes in this series. With that said, I must praise the various non-fiction histories that contributed to the background of this book including *Roman Empire* by Nigel Rodgers; *Legions of Rome* by Stephen Dando-Collins; and the exceptionally stunning biography, *Augustus First Emperor of Rome* by Adrian Goldsworthy. All these books, among many others, offer a wonderful insight into the history and world of the Roman Empire.

The glory that was Rome!

ABOUT THE AUTHOR

GARY LOVISI is a Brooklyn, New York based writer, editor, publisher and book collector. He has written fiction and non-fiction in almost every genre and has been nominated for a Mystery Writer's of America Edgar Award for the Best Short Story of the Year, as well as receiving a Western Writer's of America Spur Award for his editorial work in the Western historical genre. He has been a reader and researcher of historical fiction of all kinds, but focusing on the American Civil War, the Napoleonic Era, and The Roman Empire as key interests. His book, *Modern Historical Adventure Novels* (Gryphon Books, 2006) is a large-size, non-fiction, detailed survey, index and value guide to all the many books that have been published in this genre over the last five decades.

His interest in the Roman Empire began publication in the fiction realm with his series about young Gaetano Salvidienus Rufus, in the book, **THE SicilliAN #1: AUGUSTUS, THE UNDEFEATED** published by Wildside Books, in a 2017 trade paperback, with cover art by Marcus Boas. That is the first book in his Sicillian / Augustus Roman series, followed now by **THE SicilliAN: BOOK 2: AUGUSTUS THE CONQUEROR** (Wildside Books, trade paperback, order from www.wildsidepress.com. You can find out more about Lovisi and his work at his website, gryphonbooks.com, or his Facebook page, and you can also view his videos on rae books and book collecting on his Youtube channel.

ABOUT THE COVER ARTIST

MARCUS BOAS is a New York City illustrator, a master of vivid fantasy and science fiction art. His use of striking colors and heroic images is a mainstay used on many books and magazines in the illustration field over his decades long career. He has also done the covers on all five of the books in Gary Lovisi's Jon Kirk of Ares science fiction series. You can see more of his outstanding work collected in such books as *Heroic Fantasy*, *Jungle*, and others published by Kaso Comics at www.kasocomics.com. Wonderful prints are available for some of his beautiful work.